MATSURI AND MURDER

MISO COZY MYSTERIES
BOOK 6

STEPH GENNARO

ONIGIRI PRESS

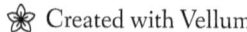

MATSURI AND MURDER

This book is dedicated to tempura.
My favorite meal on my last trip to Japan.

———

FOREWORD

In Japanese, the most common way of showing respect to another person's social standing is with the use of honorific suffixes that are appended on the end of either first or last names. The most common, -san, means either Mr., Ms., or Mrs.

In earlier versions of this book, and in the whole series, I did use these honorific suffixes. But for 2019 and onward, I have switched to the English way in order to make this series more accessible to English speakers. I hope you enjoy this version!

The town in this novel, Chikata, is completely fictional, though the area I put it in is not. Saitama prefecture is located to the west of Tokyo, and many of the eastern areas are considered to be suburbs of the city. Chikata is located farther out west, nearer to the prefectures of Nagano and Gunma.

CHAPTER
ONE

"*The next stop on this train is Kubako. Kubako. Doors will open on the left side of the train. The next stop on this train is Kubako...*"

The scenery outside the window of the *shinkansen* slowed down from a blurry stretch of green and brown to distinct houses and streets, and the sign over the exit blinked with the same information on the announcement. Kubako was next, and I was in for a three-day weekend of relaxation with my girlfriends.

Akiko yawned and stretched in the seat next to me, coming out of a short cat nap she had executed while in the last hour of our trip. I admired her ability to nap anywhere at any time. Really, it was a gift. One I wished I had now that I was in my third trimester of pregnancy. The vibrations of the train had kept my in utero baby girl quiet during our four-hour trip, but I could not sleep. Typical.

Rubbing her face and raking her fingers through her shoulder-length hair, Akiko sighed and closed her eyes again. She just needed another moment to come back to consciousness.

I glanced across our three seats to Kayo, my friend who had invited me on this little weekend getaway. Her fingers flicked in and out of her hair, and she chewed on the ends as she poured over her pile of papers. She was still mired in police work though we were hundreds of kilometers from home. She may have gotten the days off from the precinct, but that didn't mean she couldn't work while she was traveling.

"Get enough done?" I asked, reaching to the floor below Akiko in the middle to pick up the food bag. I groaned trying to maneuver around my belly.

Kayo popped out of her thoughts as she looked over the papers. "Oh, Mei, let me get that for you." She dropped her pen, and it rolled away. Akiko snapped her hand out and caught it before it ended up on the floor.

"I'm awake. I'm awake," she said, laughing and blinking her eyes hard.

Kayo grabbed the bag and promptly smacked her head on the tray table as she surfaced. All of her papers jumped and the pen Akiko had just rescued hit the floor, anyway.

Kayo sank back into her seat and closed her eyes. "I need this vacation more than anything."

Akiko and I exchanged glances.

"You don't say? Well, for starters," Akiko said, gathering up Kayo's paperwork, "you need to put this away. It's not a vacation if you're doing work the whole time."

I grabbed Kayo's folder and held it open while Akiko unceremoniously shoved the papers into it.

"I know, I know. It's just... there's a lot of work back home, and I don't want to fall behind. I really want that promotion, and I..." Her voice trailed off as she looked out the window and saw her hometown come into view. "We're almost there."

It had been her idea to travel to Kubako this weekend. Her

hometown is well-known throughout Mie prefecture for their early October *matsuri,* a festival celebrating a local historical monk, and she hadn't attended the matsuri in years. Her parents had begged her to come, and she finally said yes after they agreed to host Akiko and me as well. But I knew deep down inside she'd wanted to stay home in Chikata for the long weekend and get ahead on her piles of work.

I reached across the table and squeezed her hand. "Come on. Let's try to have a little fun this weekend. I won't be drinking with you all, but I will be eating for two. And oh, I can't wait for festival food." I rubbed my belly, making Kayo smile, which was the intention. If there was one thing this pregnancy was good for, it was turning on the charm. I was often flighty, and I made tons of horrible decisions, but no one could deny a pregnant woman her food.

The train slowed even more, and Kayo shook herself out of her thoughts.

"Right. Food, drinks, sitting in hot water, relaxation. That's what we're here for." She jammed the folder full of papers into her bag, stored the tray table, and slid out from her seat. "And to see my parents. I hope they behave themselves this weekend."

Akiko and I smiled at each other as we followed Kayo up the aisle to the doors. Akiko shrugged.

"I'm sure they'll be fine," I reassured her.

After all, who could be worse than my own mother? She loved to pry into strangers lives and then insisted on feeding everyone at every moment despite having trouble seeing her own knife in front of her.

Kayo's parents would be fine.

I had no worries.

All I had were daydreams of a matsuri full of food and

games, wandering the streets of a new town, going sightseeing, watching a musical performance, and enjoying fireworks on the beach. I would miss my husband, Yasahiro, fiercely, but this was my chance to spend time with my girlfriends.

It was going to be awesome.

I was sure of it.

A COMPACT RED CAR IDLED IN THE PARKING LOT AS WE exited the train station, and an older man in black samurai army gear, donning a helmet secured with a chin strap, waited next to it. Kayo's sigh was bone deep as she spotted him and he waved to her.

"Dad," she said, her voice full of warning, "are you heading off to war?"

I held back my smile as he came to a sharp bow. "Kayo! My baby girl! You know I always get together with my friends on Fridays." He reached out for Kayo's bag. "Big plans. Big plans. We've been preparing for the Battle of Okehazama for weeks. There are only two more scenes to build!"

Kayo didn't explain. "Dad, these are my friends, Mei Suga and Akiko Kano. Mei should sit up front since she's pregnant."

We bowed to him, and he bowed back. "It's nice to meet you both. Welcome! Please call me Taro." He threw out his arms and beamed like he was welcoming a crowd of people, then he popped the trunk.

"Thank you, Mr. Mitsuwara," Akiko and I said as we hefted our weekend bags to the back of the car. Kayo's dad rushed ahead of us, slipping through us both. We paused as he leaned into the trunk and pushed stuff aside to make room for our bags.

"I, uh, forgot to empty my supplies before coming here."

I watched as he shifted cans of paint, tiny pieces of wood, fake grass, and moss to the side and back of the trunk.

"What's all this for?" I asked, trying to make polite conversation. I had seen supplies like this at my local art supply store whenever I was there to buy canvases or paint.

Painting was my favorite hobby, and I fit in as much of it as I could between running my tea shop and helping my mother clean up her belongings from our family house. About two months ago, a massive typhoon hit our town in central Japan and destroyed my childhood home. Most everything had been salvaged, but we still had plenty to find in the muck before the house was bulldozed in November and the land handed over to the grocery store chain that had been buying up property all over town. I was sad to see it all go and sad as well to find so many things damaged. This weekend away would be good for me.

Kayo jumped forward at me and held out her hands.

"Don't get him started if you want any semblance of peace this weekend."

I narrowed my eyes at Kayo and shook my head. It was so unlike her to be rude or to hush anyone, but her father just laughed as he slammed the trunk shut.

"She's right, of course. Always the smart one. Get in, and I'll tell you on the way to the house." He lifted one finger into the air. "Onward!" he called, crossing to the right side.

Kayo rolled her eyes and sighed. "You'll be sorry, Mei. Let me be the first to say 'I told you so' when we arrive at my parents' house and he's still talking about his figurines."

"Figurines?" I thought maybe he was into model house building, but I guessed figurines wasn't a stretch.

The car's horn honked twice, and I jolted backwards. But

Kayo's Dad waved out the window at a car rolling by and that driver waved back.

"Dad," Kayo hissed at him, "don't scare Mei. She's going to give birth to her baby right in the front seat."

I laughed as I got in. "I will not."

"Sorry," Taro said. He checked his watch and said the time aloud. "Let's see if I can beat my best time."

What? I had no time to ask because as soon as I buckled my belt, we sped away.

CHAPTER
TWO

Kayo's dad drove like a dragon firing its way through an epic battle, and he kept talking the entire time. The streets of Kubako were barely wide enough to fit two cars across, but that didn't stop him from tearing through town at top speed.

"We build war scenes with fully detailed figurines and horses and landscapes, and then we take a whole weekend to put them together for everyone to see. Then we act them out." He gestured to himself in all black, and the samurai helmet wedged between his legs and the car door. "Full battle gear. My armor is at home, of course."

"Dad's famous," Kayo said while trying to temper her dry tone with a smile. The smile was brief.

"I'm not famous. Your mother's the famous one." He came to a jerking halt at a traffic light, and I whipped my hand out to stop myself from slamming into the car's console.

"Dad! Gentle! Mei's husband will kill me if anything happens to her."

"Sorry!" He didn't sound sorry. He actually sounded

amused. "Kayo's been trying to get me to ease up on my driving for twenty years. About as long as I've been making figurines."

Taro threw the car into gear and tore away from the light so fast our wheels squealed on the pavement.

"It's just not in my nature!" he yelled over the roaring engine.

I glanced over my shoulder at Akiko in the backseat next to Kayo. Her face was pale, and she gripped the car door handle so hard her knuckles were white.

Was it too much to ask for a little less drama when away from home? I used to believe my hometown, Chikata, was the most boring place in the world. And then I moved back there, and it'd been nothing but murders and scandals since. But maybe Kayo's father's driving was the worst of it?

For once, I couldn't let my mind wander and think about something else. My daydreaming time on the train would have to tide me over until I was no longer in a car with a driver determined to kill us.

"Almost there!" He flung the car into the next gear and pressed the accelerator into the floor.

A squeak escaped as my daughter somersaulted in my belly. Maybe she loved all this excitement? My heart hammered away, and I gasped as we took a corner so fast I swore two of the tires left the road. The baby punched my bladder. Yeah, she was a daredevil. How awesome for me. I mean, I loved mysteries and running after someone who had broken the law, but I drew the line at being run over by a bear and tasered in the leg.

And risky driving.

Taro turned onto a quiet road and bounced down the rural avenue for a few houses before careening into a driveway and screeching to a stop. Akiko squeaked, and I gripped the console in front of me, attempting to secure myself in one spot.

Kayo's dad checked his watch. "Six minutes, twenty-two seconds." He sighed as he opened the door. "I lost precious seconds going through town."

"There was a town?" I asked as I slid from the car. My knees were weak, and I nearly crawled away.

Akiko exited and stood next to the car, her hand on the trunk and her head down. "Don't puke. Don't puke," she repeated to herself at a whisper. She righted herself and walked towards me on wobbly legs. "You okay?" And then she did what she always does. She reached for my wrist to check my pulse. No one could stop the nurse in Akiko, not even Kayo's daredevil driving father.

"I'll be okay. Eventually."

Kayo exited the car and popped the trunk to grab our bags. Akiko and I watched her with open mouths. She wasn't even a little fazed. Not a tremble. Not a whimper. She set our bags on the driveway and slammed the trunk closed before noticing us.

"Oh, are you both all right? Dad's a little crazy with the driving."

"A little?" Akiko's voice cracked.

She shrugged. "He used to drive the fire engine back when it was all volunteers. Quickest driver in all of Mie Prefecture," she intoned like she had heard it every day her entire life.

"Kayo!" A woman called from the house, and this time Kayo cringed.

Akiko and I both turned to see Kayo's... mother? I wasn't sure until she got closer. Her hair was bright, peony pink, a color I've only seen on teenagers or in a garden. And her clothing? I termed this style "colorful layers," a style I had seen recently in trendier places in Harajuku. She wore a pink and white striped tank top under a ripped, darker pink shirt, another pink hooded sweatshirt over that. Her legs were a blur of pink flowered leggings under a pink ruffled peasant skirt.

Pink, pink, pink.

She wore more pink than I thought I even owned.

Kayo pressed her lips together and nodded her head as her mother tore across the front garden towards her. "Pink," was all she said before her mother wrapped her in a warm hug and rocked her side to side.

"Ah, it's good to see you, my baby girl," she said, pulling away from Kayo and holding Kayo's face between her two hands. Her fingers were covered in jewelry.

"Not such a baby anymore, Mom," Kayo said, and I detected the note of bittersweetness in her voice. She wasn't annoyed so much as sad.

I shifted between my feet before I leaned my shoulder on Akiko. Akiko had no family anymore. With both her parents and brother dead, I was her only close family. And I had plenty of my own family to deal with too. My mother was strict, private, and yet overbearing, and my brother always conveniently forgot that I was a member of the family.

Families were complicated, and I was sure Kayo's was as typical as anyone else's.

"These must be your friends," Kayo's mom called out, extending her arms to Akiko and me. She glided up to us and bowed before grabbing our bags. "Let me get these for you. Welcome, ladies. We're happy to have you here this weekend."

"Thank you for having us, Mrs. Mitsuwara," Akiko said with a bow. "Let me help with the bags." She dove forward to grab her bag, but Kayo's mom pulled it away.

"Nope. I'm a strong woman. I can carry these. And please

call me Hana. None of that formality stuff around my house. I've always been a little too carefree for ceremony."

I glanced at Kayo, and I now saw her in an entirely new light. These were the parents who had raised her? Kayo was always the picture of civility. She was a rules-follower, always on time, and never a crease or seam out of place on her police uniform. I'd never seen her wear any other color other than white, gray, or black.

Kayo made eye contact with me for a moment before shaking her head and laughing.

"Now you know why I've never introduced you to my family before."

"Uh, no... I mean, yes, uh..." I stammered as I walked next to her towards the house. "Your parents seem like fine people."

Kayo's face fell, her expression neutral. "They're all certifiably insane."

Her deadpan voice made me giggle nervously, and I sighed as I followed behind her.

Well, at least this weekend would be far from boring.

———

WE WEREN'T STAYING IN THE MITSUWARA HOUSE FOR THE weekend since the house was so small. Instead, we would check in at the guesthouse right next door after 15:00. Seeing as it was before noon, though, we freshened up and prepared to head out for lunch and to see the town. A beautiful day and a warm weekend laid ahead of us. October in Japan could either be rainy and chilly or warm and sunny. We were lucky to get the latter.

Kayo's old room wasn't hers anymore. Her mother had turned the place into a sewing and crafting room. I jumped as I entered the sliding door and found colorful wigs on mannequin heads staring me in the face.

"Well, that solves that mystery," I mumbled to Akiko.

"I had wondered if that was her own hair." Akiko placed her bag next to mine and then stood up to turn and examine the room.

Color covered everything. It was as if two rainbows had mated in this room and had many, many babies. Ribbons, thread, and stacks of fabric were piled into bookcases along one wall. The room's closet door was open and clear plastic bins full of sewing notions occupied every shelf inside. A giant worktable sat against the wall opposite the room's door, and a sewing machine and a serger awaited use. I was familiar with these tools though I couldn't sew a straight line to save my life. Mom had dabbled in sewing for most of my youth. We had been poor, and making and repairing our kimonos was something she enjoyed doing.

But despite the chaos of the colorful room, everything was neat and tidy. A folded, bright green blanket sat on the back of a recliner chair in the corner, a stack of fashion and sewing books next to it. The floor was open, and the tatami mats in here had been vacuumed recently. I noticed that the trash bin overflowed with scraps and threads, no doubt cleared from the work table. Kayo's mom, Hana, seemed to take care of the house and herself.

This meshed with what I knew of Kayo. Kayo's apartment was always tidy and clean every time I had been there in the last year. Her apartment was also modern, with dark and classy furniture. Nothing like we'd seen so far in the house.

Kayo followed us into the room, calling over her shoulder down the hall. "We'll be right there, Mom!"

She walked in the room, took one look around, nodded and dumped her bag on the floor next to ours.

"So, let's get changed and then we'll head out to the town center for lunch and festival food, okay?" Kayo paused and stared at the recliner chair for a long moment before shaking out of her thoughts and squatting next to her bag. Her eyes creased at the corners, and her movements were crisp and practiced. I recognized the signs of stress; I'd had them often enough. Kayo was not exactly happy to be home.

This trip had been her idea though. She'd brought it up during one of our girls' night out dinners, how her hometown has this matsuri every October and how much she missed it and missed her family. In the next breath, she suggested we should all go. And she even made all the plans, booked the train tickets, and the inn.

"Is everything okay?" I would squat down next to her, but my pregnant belly made that problematic, so I rested my hand on her shoulder. Seeing Kayo like this unnerved me. She was the rock in our group, the port in the storm. She always had her head clear, her mind focused. When my brain traveled off on a vacation to dreamland, she paid attention.

"Fine. Everything's fine." She grabbed a new shirt and stood up. "For once, I'm home, and everything's just the way it should be." She jerked her thumb at the door. "I'm going to get changed in the bathroom and wash up. Let's all meet out front in fifteen minutes."

CHAPTER
THREE

Out in the front garden, Hana, Kayo's mom, was in the middle of a photo shoot. She stood among the fall flowers and fading greenery of October while Akiko took her photo again and again.

"Turn a little to your left," Akiko instructed, holding the phone camera out and snapping a few more photos.

Hana had the poses down like rote memory. She did a stand-tall pose before she turned to the side and kicked out her leg. I watched with polite amusement, entranced by this woman who so clearly did not care what anyone thought of her. She was still young for having such older children, and she loved every second of it. Maybe it was nothing to be amused by, but I tried to picture myself in the same position in fifteen to twenty years, and I figured it would be a miracle if I ever wore anything even semi-fashionable now, much less in a decade or two.

"You look great," Akiko said, handing Hana's phone back to her.

"Thanks. Ah!" she cried, smiling at the photos. "You did an excellent job. These will be popular on Instagram."

I brightened up. "We should follow each other! I take photos at my husband's restaurant and at my tea shop."

"Yes, let's do that." She crowded up next to me so we could see each other's accounts on our phones. I typed in her username and nearly choked on my own tongue. She had over twenty thousand followers! And my four hundred looked measly next to hers.

"Wow," I said, breathing out a surprised sigh, "you have so many followers!" I scrolled through her feed and ogled at the numbers. Some of her photos had over thirty-thousand likes and oodles of comments. But her style was so fun and vibrant, and based on the pictures she'd posted, she changed colors often, and sometimes even dressed down. She took her style seriously, and it showed.

She waved her hand at me. "It's the colorful outfits. People love them."

So I guessed she was famous after all.

Kayo joined us and led us back in the direction of town. No more driving, thank the heavens. I'd rather walk, even as pregnant as I was.

We passed our hotel for the next few nights. Its front garden was so beautiful and quiet with a koi pond and wooden lanterns leading the way to the dark wood front deck.

"The inn is managed by my childhood best friend's family and has been in their family for four generations. They have a really nice indoor hot spring bath that we can all enjoy later tonight, I'm sure. Plus saké from my family's brewery."

"Where is the brewery? I've forgotten the name." Akiko snapped her fingers.

"It's another three blocks," Kayo said, pointing down the

street. I craned my neck and saw a formidable, dark building with a *sugidama*, a large cedar ball, hanging outside. That was a sure sign saké was being made inside. "And it's called Imagawa. Grandpa named it after Imagawa Yoshimoto, the daimyō who lost the Battle of Okehazama to Nobunaga."

"I'm impressed with your command of history." I adjusted my bag and sniffed the air. Fried food! My stomach grumbled. "I don't remember any of the names of the warlords from history class."

Kayo shrugged. "It's Dad's thing, and my older brother's passion too. He teaches at a university in Hokkaido. My older sister and Mom do the fashion thing. And I..." Her voice trailed off. "Anyway, we'll go eat and then we'll come back to the brewery for drinks and snacks later. Dad and Fumio are having an open house, and usually the place is hopping with people. We won't want to miss it."

We passed the Imagawa brewery and kept going to the main street. The local police had the road blocked off, and people were streaming in and out of the barricades. Kayo spoke to a few of the officers she knew, and while she was talking, Akiko, Hana, and I moved along to determine what we would eat first.

"Oh, takoyaki!" Akiko pointed to a stall making savory dough balls with chopped octopus in them. One of my personal favorites.

"Yes, and then the grilled chicken too." My mouth watered considering my options. "With rice."

"Of course. Let's get in line." Akiko looked between Hana and me, but Hana shook her head.

"I'm going to start with a salad first. I've been craving greens all day, and this stall over here is run by a nearby farm just out of town." She pointed to a stall next to the takoyaki one we were heading to. "They make a wild mushroom and greens salad with local ingredients. It's one of my favorites."

"Oh, I want that too," I groaned, suddenly so hungry I could eat everything in front of us.

Hana laughed. "I'll get in line for salads for all of us."

Akiko and I stepped into the takoyaki line, and by my estimate, it looked like we would wait about ten minutes. Not too bad. Akiko's phone buzzed, so she sighed and attended to whatever needed her attention, and I did what I did best. I daydreamed.

I imagined Kayo growing up in this town. In my thoughts, she was a young teenager, shouldering her backpack, and walking up and down the street, to and from school. Her little quirk of a sarcastic smile would light up the clerks at the convenience store as she picked up food for her mom and dad after a long day of studying. On the weekends, she would do her homework at the saké brewery while her dad worked or help him with tasks like steaming the rice or labeling the bottles. In my head, the scene was idyllic and happy.

"Mei," Akiko said, smacking my arm, "you're not listening to a word I'm saying."

"Sorry! Sorry. I was... in my head. What did you say?"

Akiko blinked at me a few times as we shifted forward in the line.

"Another one of my clients has decided to move into the assisted living facility in town." She frowned as she dropped her phone in her bag. "I feel bad that I'm not there."

"Don't," I said, resting my hand on her arm. As a traveling nurse, Akiko's main clients were almost all elderly patients, and many of them had become my friends and clients as well. Back when I desperately needed work, Akiko had introduced me to several of them, and I helped them in return for small wages until I was back on my feet. Now I ran a tea shop where most of my elderly clients could rest and socialize outside of their apartments. "Is it anyone I know?"

"No, but I must introduce you when we return home. I think she'd enjoy time at the tea shop."

I nodded as Kayo approached. Her cheeks had grown rosy while talking to the local police officers.

"It's nice out today." She turned around to check the lines then leaned into us. "Oh, look. The woman in front of my mom at the salad stall? She's the lead flutist at the festival show tomorrow night."

Akiko and I slowly turned our heads so we could spot this woman. Wow. She was a stunner. Her hair was jet black, straight and shiny, and her skin was a glorious pale white. I could never achieve that kind of color no matter how hard I tried. Even with the wide-brimmed hats and elbow-length gloves I wore all summer, I still got too much sun to be so fair.

"She's an amazing performer, and she's been one of the stars of the festival for five years running. Isn't she gorgeous?" We looked again at Kayo's insistence. The woman smiled politely at the older couple speaking to her in line. "I heard she was auditioning for some NHK period drama, too."

"What's her name?"

"Juno Takagi. Watch out for her. I'm sure she'll be a star someday."

I glanced over Kayo's shoulder to get a better look at Juno. I watched all the period dramas either on TV with Akiko or online when things were slow at the tea shop. If this woman was going to be a star, I wanted to keep an eye on her career. Yasahiro hated the fuss over celebrities (he was a celebrity himself at one point), but I loved a good TV show. I concentrated on actors, and that was about it.

Juno struck up a conversation with Kayo's mom, and she and Hana were laughing about something as they approached the front of the line. The young lady handling the salad orders paused as Juno gave her order. Her eyes widened, and she appeared to become star struck. I smiled as I watched her fumble around in the stall and hand over a plastic container of salad. Another young woman, wearing a kerchief on her head and glasses, placed her hand on the shoulder of the young lady and handed over a small plastic cup of dressing. Juno smiled and thanked them, paid, and left, waving to Hana as she walked away. She met up with a handsome man her own age a few stalls farther into the festival, and the two disappeared into the crowd.

It was our turn to order our lunch, and we stepped up to the stall to get our takoyaki. With the salads Hana had purchased, we had an excellent start to the food portion of our little vacation. Down the street, we passed stalls with ice cream and *dango*, sweet rice balls on a stick covered with a sweet, sticky sauce. My mouth watered as we walked by. Kayo and Hana found an empty bench off the main street just as the sun came out, and we ate in the warm October sun with green tea from the convenience store across the street.

After our bellies were full, Akiko leaned back in the bench and tipped her face to the sun.

"Ahhh, this is lovely. It's nice not to be at the beck and call of my patients for once."

"Or Kirin," I said, mentioning her dog.

"Kirin is enjoying a weekend at the expensive doggy spa. I'm sure she's more than happy to be rid of me for a bit." Akiko smiled, even though Kirin was her only family now. "What's on the agenda for the rest of the day?"

"We're going to walk the length of the stalls and get more

food, then we'll shove off to the brewery. I had Dad reserve us a table because many of the people here will bring their food back to Imagawa to eat and drink. We could've done that, but I wanted to show you more of the town."

I would never complain about walking and sightseeing, even with a baby belly to contend with. Walking was my favorite activity, and I walked a lot at home too. Before long, we had dessert, and we were exploring the nearby temple grounds when Kayo's phone rang.

"It's Dad," she said, swiping the phone screen. She pressed the phone to her ear. "Hi, Dad. Dad?" She paused for a long moment, so I turned from admiring the intricate wall carvings along the outside of the main temple. Kayo's eyebrows pulled together as she listened to her father. "Okay. Okay. We'll get right over there."

She hung up and swore under her breath.

"What's wrong?" I could feel the energy riding up under my skin. The only calls that were that short and that terse were the ones that brought bad news.

"I think... I think someone's been murdered at my dad's brewery. We have to go."

CHAPTER
FOUR

The Imagawa Brewery was in chaos when we arrived. The front door slid open, and we were met with a crowd of people standing among the rows of shelved saké. Not only did Imagawa Brewery sell its own saké, but they also shelved and sold saké from other breweries in Mie Prefecture. Saké was one of my favorite drinks when I wasn't pregnant, and my mom and I often drank together in the evenings when we were done in the farm fields.

I halted the memories before I drowned in them. Mom and I'd had a tough year, and now that the family home and farm had been destroyed by a typhoon, there wouldn't be any nights on the porch, drinking saké and reminiscing.

"Stand back, Kayo. I can't let you through."

I edged through the crowd to join Kayo and Akiko who were being held back from the seating area by a police officer.

"This is my family's brewery, and I'm also a police officer," Kayo said, reaching into her bag and pulling out her badge and identification. "You will let us past."

The young man sighed and glanced over his shoulder.

"Detective Sano is here," he whispered, and Kayo raised her eyebrows.

"How did he get here so quickly?" she whispered back.

"He was having drinks with the deceased." His eyes widened, and I gasped. I had no idea who this Detective Sano was, but for someone to die right next to him? That would be a huge disgrace, utterly shameful. "So, he's not in a good mood. I don't think you should interfere."

Kayo shrugged and pushed past him.

"Don't say I didn't warn you," he mumbled as we all followed her.

My eyes did what they normally do at a crime scene, they surveyed the room.

I was impressed by the beautiful layout of the brewery and its amenities. Most breweries were just small buildings that housed the equipment for making saké — the steamers, vats, and bottling equipment. Usually, there was a room for distributing *koji*, the mold that makes the rice ferment, and then maybe a room or two for offices and staff. That was it.

But this brewery seemed to have it all. Not only did it have a store with shelves of saké, but it also sold already chilled bottles and self-serve single helpings. Then the area opposite the store was a raised platform of bright, warm wood, with sunken tables for hanging out and drinking what you bought. Windows along the wall perpendicular to the street looked out on a small garden with outdoor seating. Many people stood outside and gawked at the scene indoors.

As we approached the crime scene, I focused on the seating area. Several of the tables appeared to have been abandoned when the drama broke out. Bags of food brought in from the festival were piled on two tables, and purses and backpacks sat next to the wall. I sniffed the air and didn't notice the smell of anything cooking. Instead of being BYOB (Bring Your Own Beer), this place was probably "bring your own food." It was a business model that worked well in Tokyo, so why not here?

Kayo swore, and her frustrated tone brought my attention back to the scene at hand. "It's Juno Takagi."

Slumped to the side, her hair thrown over her face, Juno Takagi, the rising starlet and center of attention at the upcoming festival celebration tomorrow, laid dead at one of the tables.

This was not my first dead body, but I never enjoyed this part of the business... which wasn't my business either. I was a tea shop owner, not a police officer, not a detective, and not a private investigator. But for some reason, death followed me everywhere.

I was kind of getting used to it.

Kind of.

"I can't believe she's dead," a woman behind us whispered. Kayo and I turned around and faced a woman with a pale face and tear-stained cheeks. She looked familiar, but I couldn't place her.

"Chisé?" Kayo asked.

The woman nodded, a tear rolling down her cheek and catching on her bottom lip. She focused on Kayo and frowned. "Do I know you?"

"We went to school together," she said, but Chisé didn't respond. "I'm sorry about your sister."

"She complained about stomach troubles all week, and I worried she had an ulcer. But then she was fine all afternoon. I don't know what happened." She covered her mouth with her hand. "She was just drinking the saké and..." A sob bent her over.

Great. This did not sound good for the brewery. Not one bit.

"Chisé," a female police officer interrupted, "please come with me. I have a few questions for you." The officer led the sister away from everyone to question her in private. The officer nodded to Kayo, and Kayo nodded back. They must've known each other.

"Kayo." Kayo's dad grabbed her arm, squeezed, and pulled her away from the scene. Akiko and I followed. "I'm so glad you're here."

Taro's face was wan, the opposite of the bright and sunny demeanor from earlier. Though he still wore his black clothes, his samurai helmet was on a table close to the back of the sitting area. There, several other men dressed the same way murmured between each other. This must have been his band of friends that he made models and figurines with.

"What's going on, Dad?" Kayo glanced over her dad's shoulder and spotted a man in a suit questioning someone down the hall leading to the back of the brewery.

"Detective Sano is threatening to shut the whole place down. He's calling this place a crime scene, and he says Fumio and I are the main suspects." His voice climbed, but he kept his temper under control. Then he realized Akiko and I were listening in. "I'm so sorry. I know you came here to relax..." His voice quieted as he turned his wedding ring on his finger a few times.

"This is not my first murder scene," I said, trying not to sound apathetic.

"Nor mine," Akiko chimed in. "And I'm a nurse. I've seen plenty of dead bodies, but they're usually quite old." She leaned over to Kayo. "Do you think I could get a look at the body without anyone caring?"

Kayo's eyes darted side to side. Many people were leaving the brewery now that the initial scandal was dying down, and a photographer had finished taking photos of the body. Now was as good a time as any.

Reaching into her bag, Kayo produced an empty evidence bag filled with gloves.

Akiko laughed. "Always prepared."

Kayo rolled her eyes. "You have no idea. Let's go."

I let them go, and I turned to Taro. "Let's sit down and try not to worry." I placed my hand on his shoulder and tried to direct him to his table, but he shook his head.

"I'm worried about Fumio." He jerked his head at the young man being grilled by another other man in the suit.

"And Fumio is...?" I prompted, hoping to get more information on these people.

"My senior manager. He's going to buy this place from me when I retire."

I could see right away that this would not end well for Fumio. The man in the suit, Detective Sano, was at least ten centimeters taller than Fumio, and he used that to his advantage, backing Fumio against the wall and leaving him no personal space.

This was something I hated about being around the police, confrontation. At home, I didn't have this problem with the Chikata police force, especially now that the one guy who hated me was gone. We were all great friends. But this town was at least three times the size of Chikata, and it had a real detective, not someone they borrowed from Tokyo if they needed to. And I didn't know this guy Fumio at all, but I couldn't let him be bullied by some overbearing officer.

I walked straight up to them both and heard the last of

Sano's question to Fumio. "And how did you know Juno Takagi?"

Fumio sighed, and it was weary. He stroked his cheek which had at least two days' worth of beard growth. "Well, I didn't. I know who she is... was. Everyone in town knew her," he protested. Sano wrote this down in his notebook. "But I didn't *know* her. I don't even think she knew my name."

"Excuse me," I said, butting in. Both men startled and turned to me. "Hi. I'm a friend of the Mitsuwara family, and I think Fumio is needed back at his job. Are you done with him?"

Fumio startled out of his shock first. He ran his hand through his thick hair and bowed before tightening his indigo apron. "Yes, I really should be getting back to work." He reached into the front pocket of the apron and produced a business card. "You can reach me at any of these numbers or by email." Using both hands, he presented the business card to Sano, bowed, and left for the back of the brewery. Just before he closed the door, he looked over his shoulder at me, puzzled by my appearance.

"And who are you?" Sano asked me, annoyed to be interrupted.

"Ah," I said, reaching into my bag and producing my own business card. "My name is Mei Suga, and I'm in town visiting my friend's family. They happen to own this brewery."

"Who's your friend?" he asked, looking past me. "Kayo Mitsuwara?" He must've seen Kayo and Akiko looking over the body, but I didn't look over my shoulder to check. I couldn't take my eyes off of him or he'd bolt, so I stepped into his line of sight.

"Yes, Kayo. Do you know her?"

"I do," he growled. He didn't seem pleased about it. I ignored him.

"I don't want to step on any toes, but back home, I've helped solve a number of murder cases —"

"Excuse me?" he said, finally paying attention to me. "I'm not going to let civilians get involved in a murder case."

My face heated, but I stood my ground, imagining myself in a position of power I had no right even trying to claim. But something about being in a different town, a place where no one knew me as the daydreaming screw-up I had been until recently, gave me the confidence I usually didn't have.

"We don't have to get involved, but we'd like to help."

He pushed past me, his anger getting the best of him, and he stalked up to Akiko and Kayo who were bent over Juno's dead body.

"Do not touch this body," Sano demanded, pointing at Kayo and Akiko.

Akiko held up her hands. "I haven't touched her." She stood up and snapped off her gloves. "There appears to be an excessive amount of saliva in Juno Takagi's mouth." She pointed down to a small puddle of drool on the wood floor. "What happened right before she passed?"

Sano's mouth opened and closed a few times before he shot daggers from his eyes at Kayo. "You know, when you left the force here, I told you that you weren't welcome back."

I gasped again and covered my mouth. How rude.

Kayo didn't blink. I had to give it to her. She was always a rock.

"And I told you I wasn't interested in coming back. We're just visiting. But since you're accusing my father, and Fumio, of killing Miss Takagi, then I feel I must intervene on their behalf. Can you answer Akiko's question? I hear you were having drinks with Juno when she died."

Sano stood silent.

"What was she like?"

"She was a very... private... person," he ground out through a locked jaw.

"That's not what I meant, and you know it." Kayo sighed before looking around. The crowd had dispersed out through the door, and the sound of a siren approached in the distance. "I can wait for the chief to show up if I need to. He always had a soft spot for me, and this place, too. As far as I know, he still comes here to drink with my dad at least once a week."

This time, Sano softened a little, but his eyes remained focused on Kayo.

"She was fine when I picked her and her sister up at the matsuri about an hour ago. We arrived here, and we were having dessert and drinking the saké when she became pale and complained of a stomach ache. She reached across the table for the water jug and knocked it over, then she fell over, convulsed a few times, and... well, that was it. She was dead before I could do a damned thing."

Kayo looked at me, and I nodded. Poisoned, for sure. But now I had even more questions. When was she poisoned? What was she poisoned with? And why?

The siren outside peaked and turned off. The door to the brewery whooshed open and another man in a suit, flanked by several other people, strode in.

A man I had seen earlier, the one who had walked away with Juno, pushed past everyone in front of him, took two long steps, and punched Sano so hard he hit the floor and knocked over a bottle of saké. Akiko, Kayo, and I leaped out of the way while the man shook out his hand.

"Arrest him," he said, pointing at Sano who was groaning and clutching his cheek. "He murdered my girlfriend."

CHAPTER
FIVE

Hana and Taro looked stricken. They were hunched over, pale, and tired as they sat on the couch in the main office and spoke with the chief. Juno's body had been carted off. Sano had gone to the police station for questioning, and the forensics crew had done their work. The light and relaxing afternoon had morphed into a stressful situation, and the sunlight was beginning to wane.

Out in the central area, Akiko and I helped Kayo pick up the mess left behind by the incident.

"Sorry," Kayo said again, apologizing for the millionth time. "I'm not sure when they'll be done, but I don't think I should leave without Mom and Dad."

"No, of course not," Akiko said, dumping some trash into the main bin. Everything that had been evidence in the murder was gone, whisked away by the forensics team. "We should definitely stay until they can leave too. We're in no rush, right, Mei?"

I wasn't paying attention until I heard my name.

"What's that?" I asked, freezing with a stack of saké cups in my hands.

Akiko rolled her eyes at me. "Mei doesn't object. What were we going to do tonight, anyway?"

"Sit in the baths, eat, and go to bed early." I laughed at myself. "I sound like some of my elderly clients. Have I suddenly turned eighty?"

Kayo puffed air out her lips as she swept the floor. "You sound like someone almost seven months pregnant. Don't worry about it." She gathered up her piles of dirt, swept them into a dustpan, and dropped the remains in the trash. "Hey, um, I need to go talk to Fumio. Do you want to see the back of the brewery?" She grabbed a plastic bin of dirty saké cups and bottles.

Akiko sighed as she pulled her phone from her purse. "I'd love to, but I have emails to deal with. I'm going to sit outside and take care of them if you don't mind."

"I think I need to sit," I said, and Kayo's eyes widened in panic.

"Mei, can you come with me, please?"

Hmmm, what was up with Kayo? For her to ask me so intensely to do something as simple as this? It wasn't like her. She charged into every situation without fear. I couldn't refuse her. She needed me to come with her, for some reason.

"Sure."

I followed her to the hallway, throwing a glance over my shoulder at Akiko. But if she noticed Kayo acting strange, she didn't say anything.

Back in the brewery, the main room was hot and sticky. The big rice steamers were off, but it smelled like freshly cooked rice.

"I can't tell you how many hours, days, years I spent back

here, growing up," Kayo said, a bittersweet smile on her face. "My biggest chore was washing dishes." She hefted the plastic bin and jerked her chin at a kitchen setup — a sink, shelves, stove, and industrial dishwasher — at the far rear of the building.

We passed an enclosed white room with a large picture window and paused to watch the activity inside. Four men, including Fumio, were shirtless around a double meter wide and long table. They were all using their hands to spread hot rice on the table to be cooled. The process took a while, and the men worked together like a well-rehearsed ballet to smooth out the rice into a uniform level and thickness. When they were done, they were all shining with sweat and looking down at their accomplishment with pride on their faces.

I thought they were done when three of the men left the room, but Fumio stayed behind.

Kayo sighed, and it sounded a lot more lonesome than I expected from her. Her eyes never left Fumio as he got to work inside the room. He slowly circled the table of rice, shaking a metal container over the cooling grains. This was the koji mold that encouraged rice to break down and ferment into saké. I had no direct experience with saké brewing, but this wasn't the first brewery I had toured.

Watching Fumio's intense concentration as he paid attention to every single shake of the koji and where it fell on the rice was mesmerizing. He was precise about this in the way of a professional who cared deeply for his craft.

Kayo licked her bottom lip and drew in a quick breath. I knew that look. The longing stare, the measured breaths...

"Kayo, are you and Fumio...?" I didn't even know how to ask this question. Kayo had lived in Chikata, my hometown (quite far from here) for several years, and we'd been friends for just over a year. If she had been dating anyone, I would've known.

Kayo snapped out of her daze and turned away from the window, away from me. "What's that?" she asked, heading towards the kitchen sink.

"Fumio. Are you... into him?"

"It doesn't matter." She hefted her crate onto the top of the industrial dishwasher and flung open the dishwasher door. As she loaded up the bottom shelf, she kept her eyes trained downward.

"It sounds to me like it does matter." I leaned my hip against the adjacent sink. "Can I help?"

"No," she said, shaking her head. "You do enough dishes at the tea shop as it is. I just wanted you here for... for..." She stopped, her lips not finding the right words.

"Moral support? Because... you have the hots for Fumio?" I was digging, and I wasn't proud of it, but I wasn't going to stop either.

Kayo burst into a laugh. "Okay, Mei." She loaded up the last of the saké cups and held up her hands, a plea of surrender. "Fine. If you must know..." When I didn't tell her to stop, she sighed. "Fumio is my high school boyfriend. Ex-boyfriend."

"Ahhhh, I see. No wonder you didn't want to be back here with him. Why'd you break up with him?"

"Me? Break up with him?" She covered her mouth. "No. He broke up with me when he found out I got into the police academy."

My joking smile flitted away. "Oh."

"Yeah." She jabbed a few buttons on the dishwasher. "I graduated and returned here to work only to find out he was now a master brewer and due to inherit the business from my father. Sano likes to think it was his harassment that got me transferred to Chikata, but no. I left to get away from him." Kayo waved her hand at the room where Fumio was, just as the door opened and he emerged.

Kayo jumped, a little "meep" blurting from her lips. I was momentarily amused, seeing her so out of sorts, and then I chastised myself. I shouldn't be happy about my friend being uncomfortable.

Be nicer, Mei.

I sidled up next to her and whispered, "We came back here to question him?"

Kayo nodded.

"Want me to do the talking?" I asked, thinking this might help her through this awkward situation.

She paused for a brief moment and drew herself up. No, she was the strong police officer, and this situation wouldn't intimidate her. She had caught and apprehended murderers. She could handle Fumio.

At least that was what I suspected was going through her mind. It could have just been blind panic for all I knew. I loved to make guesses.

Fumio grabbed a short robe from the hook outside of the room and dressed himself as he approached. Thank goodness, too, because I was sure Kayo wouldn't be happy to question him with his shirt off.

"Kayo, I thought you'd be gone by now." He barely let his eyes rest on her before he smiled politely at me. "I'm sorry we didn't meet earlier, and thank you for getting Sano off my case." He bowed, and I returned it. "That man is... Well, he's aggressive, but I guess all police officers are."

Kayo's lips pinched into an X. Hmmm, I never thought of her as the aggressive type. Sure, she's strong-willed and gets the job done, but aggressive? Only when apprehending a criminal.

"He seemed to be questioning you for no good reason, so I thought I'd step in. I'm Mei Suga, a friend of Kayo's from Chikata. It's nice to meet you." We bowed and shook hands.

"Fumio Noguchi."

I filed away his name for later. "Our other friend, Akiko, is outside on the phone."

Fumio went to the fridge down the counter from the sink and pulled out a bottle of water.

"You came here at the right time. The festival is a lot of fun." He paused, his eyebrows drawing together. "But, huh, I wonder what will happen now that the star flute player has passed away."

"The show will go on. It always does," Kayo said, breaking into our conversation. "It worked fine for years before Juno showed up to be the star."

"Did she not grow up here?" I asked. I was growing more curious about this woman as the day wore on. Speaking of which, my hips and feet were beginning to hurt.

"No. Her family moved here in high school. Then she dated the most popular boy in school. You can probably guess the rest."

Dated the most popular boy and maybe several more since. I saw her at the festival with the man who punched Sano. Had they really been dating?

Inside my chest, the desire to solve a mystery grew and fluttered, like a butterfly punching out of its cocoon. But I was far from home and a police force that knew me and trusted me. How would we solve a murder here with very little help?

The old-fashioned way, by being nosy busybodies with nothing else to do. Prying into other people's lives was not really in our nature, nor a part of our culture, but lives were on the line! (I imagined myself raising my fist in the air.)

"Not that Kayo was jealous or anything," Fumio said, and I widened my eyes at this. It was mentioned in jest, but Kayo's previous mood suggested she was far from being interested in jokes.

She barked a short laugh. "Me? Jealous? I was already dating someone if you don't remember."

He gulped down his water and spun the cap back on the bottle. "I remember."

My baby belly moved as if to prompt me to get on with the conversation. I wondered again whether this little girl would end up being my sidekick in the years to come.

"Can you tell me about the time before she died? Just here, in the brewery? Were you around?" I asked, jumping in before the silence could get too uncomfortable.

"I was," he replied. He finished his water bottle, crushed it, and chucked it in the recycling. Kayo watched each movement, her eyes bouncing back and forth. "The rice was still steaming, and the front store was crawling with people, so I offered to help out. I had been visiting each table, speaking with the customers, pouring saké..." He shrugged, indicating he was doing the usual things that were expected of him. "Sano and Juno had been speaking. I noticed she didn't look well. She was paler than usual, and her hands trembled as she tried to pour saké for Sano. She apologized and waved me over to clean up the table which I was happy to do. I had a rag just for such things."

He paused, and his eyes seemed to be focused far off down the hall toward the front room.

"Sano joked with me something like, 'What do you put in this saké? Drugs?' or something like that." He shook his head. "I have never liked that guy. He's too brash, too impolite."

His eyes flicked at Kayo, and I wondered if Sano had been that way to Kayo and that's why it bothered Fumio. I wasn't going to ask.

"Anyway, I was on my way back here when I heard a shout, and the next thing I knew, Juno was slumped over unconscious. I ran over to help, but she convulsed a few times, and then..."

Then she was dead.

"It's such a shame. She was a very kind person, accomplished. Her family is well-known here."

Kayo jumped into the conversation. "Did Sano accuse you or Dad of poisoning Juno?"

Fumio laughed. "What *didn't* he accuse us of? He went on and on about how healthy Juno was and how she started feeling ill as soon as she was at the brewery. He took samples of all the saké, the water, and any snacks that had been out. He even confiscated our cups."

Kayo sighed. "Whenever I worked with him, he was always following the wrong leads in investigations. And then he'd jump into someone else's work and act like it was his idea from the start." She turned from Fumio to me. "This is the main reason why I left. He took credit for three investigations I did, and I had had enough."

Fumio's eyebrows knit. "Your mother told me you were fired and reassigned."

Kayo didn't acknowledge Fumio's statement, and I opened my mouth to question her about it. Didn't she just tell me she left Kubako to get away from Fumio? Maybe she left for a lot of reasons. She grabbed my elbow and ushered me away from Fumio.

"Thanks for the information," she called over her shoulder to him, then she leaned closer as we left Fumio behind. "Anything Sano is doing, I want to explore the opposite. So let's go get checked in at the hotel and consider our options. Tomorrow, we snoop."

I smiled at her, and she smiled back. "I like the way you think."

CHAPTER
SIX

did not want to get out of bed, but Kayo was insistent that we get going early.

"Come on," she said, tying her short hair back into a tiny ponytail. "If we get to the stands as they're setting up, we won't be bothering anyone. And we still need to have breakfast."

She waved to the table in the middle of the room, set up with a traditional Japanese breakfast. Miso soup, grilled fish, rice, and pickles awaited eating. I groaned, thinking about the pancakes Yasahiro usually made me on the weekends. Traditional Japanese breakfast just wasn't my thing. It had been my mom's thing when I was growing up. I much preferred my husband's idea of a traditional French breakfast. Pastries and coffee were more my speed.

"Fine." I threw off the covers of my floor futon. I had to roll over onto all fours and hoist myself up to standing from there. My baby belly always got in the way of things, but I tried not to wish it away. It would be gone soon enough.

I imagined myself not pregnant anymore with a toddler to run after, and I smiled.

"What are you smiling at?" Akiko asked, entering the room from the bathroom. Everyone was up but me.

"Oh, just daydreaming again."

I yawned as I lowered myself again at the table and sipped at the miso soup. Whatever we did after this, coffee had to be involved. I drank a cup of half-caf every morning despite the bad looks I got from other people. It was amazing how judgmental people were with pregnant women.

A knock at the door preceded the inn's proprietress, Manari Haségawa, entering with her daughter, Utako.

"Everyone's up! I hope you all slept well."

"We did, thanks, Mrs. Haségawa." Kayo zipped up her bag and sat down next to me.

"Can I get you anything else?" Haségawa hovered over the table, her hands clasped together. She was an attentive inn manager, and I knew from Kayo's mother that they had owned the place for several generations. They were also good friends.

"Coffee?" I asked. "Half-caf, if you have it."

"Of course! We have everything," Haségawa said, her smile growing. "So silly of me to forget the coffee service."

"I brought it, Mom." Utako set her tray down on the floor next to the table and poured coffee. Thank goodness. I was wondering where the coffee shops or convenience stores were in town if I didn't get coffee soon.

"I was hoping you ladies had some information about what happened at Imagawa Brewery yesterday. There's been talk in town."

This caught my attention, and I set down the bowl of soup. Once my hand was free, Utako floated the cup of coffee straight into it.

"Milk? Sugar?"

"Both, thanks. What have you heard?"

Kayo leaned forward over the table as she picked at her bowl of rice and fish. Even Akiko, not known for liking mysteries, paid attention.

"Juno had been seen earlier in the day with her ex-boyfriend, Seiji Sugimoto." Utako wiggled her eyebrows excited to be giving out this information.

I remembered what Kayo said yesterday. Today, we would snoop.

"You don't say." I held out my coffee cup for milk and sugar until I was happy with both. When I took a deep sniff of the cup, the baby rolled over in my belly, ready for her caffeine infusion.

Utako nodded. "Mmm-hmm. Supposedly, they were this close" — she brought her index finger and thumb together — "to getting back together. Seiji got a well-paying job in Tokyo, and Juno was going to go with him. Start up her acting career."

"What about Sano, then?" Kayo interrupted. "We heard he was dating Juno."

"He might have been," Utako breathed out, her eyes aglow with gossip. "Mind if I sit?"

"Utako!" Her mother admonished her. "We don't bother our guests while they eat breakfast."

Kayo rolled her eyes. "How long have we known each other?"

"Our entire lives," Utako said, and her mother shrugged in response.

I jostled my butt over and gestured to the space next to me. "Both of you, please stay. We were hoping to dig more into the murder today."

"Are you sure it's murder?" Utako asked, sitting down.

"I've seen enough murders to know," Kayo said.

Akiko huffed. "Most of the dead people I run across have died of old age, thankfully. Most..." She distracted herself, and my heart ached for her pain. Finding her own father murdered at home would be a wound that would take a long time to heal if it ever did.

"Then maybe it was a lover's quarrel?" Utako raised her finger in the air.

"Maybe she was going to reunite with Seiji, and then they fought because she was dating Sano," I said, feeling this theory gel in my head. I could see the scene now. Juno and Seiji, their love for each other was strong, but not strong enough to handle Sano as well.

"Or maybe she was going to go back with Seiji, and it was Sano who was devastated and killed her."

"I don't know. He seemed furious about it, don't you think?" Akiko asked, plucking another pickle from the plate next to the rice. I sipped my coffee and ignored the food. I should've been eating, but nothing appealed to me before coffee.

Kayo waved, dismissing Akiko's statement. "Sano gets angry over anything. He once yelled at an assistant for turning in a report five minutes late, and she quit the next day. Then I saw him throw his cup of coffee at a barista for getting his name wrong. The man is a pig. Total hot head. I have no idea what Juno saw in him... if they even dated."

"You think they hadn't been?" I asked.

She shrugged again.

"Oh no, something was definitely going on between them," Utako insisted. "Everyone in town talked about it, for weeks." She sat back as she looked at the table. "Mei, let me make you a bowl for breakfast." She leaned past me and got to the task before I could even deny her. I waited as she loaded up a bowl with rice, pickles, a piece of fish, and some chopped up omelet. "You must have some of this soy sauce. It's made locally."

She blushed, and I wondered who at the soy sauce shop she was interested in. In my head, he was tall and handsome. Then I imagined my own husband cooking in his kitchen, and homesickness twisted my belly. I had only been gone a day!

But it was a crazy day.

"Thanks," I said, keeping my hormones at bay as she set the bowl in front of me.

"Still," Kayo continued, getting back to the conversation, "just because everyone thought they were dating doesn't mean they were."

"I don't know." Utako shook her head. "That seems like a stretch. I had seen them both at Imagawa having drinks and looking mighty cozy."

As I conveyed the food in the bowl to my mouth, I noticed that Haségawa remained sitting on her knees, quiet and contemplative. She hadn't weighed in on this topic.

But something about her expression led me to believe she knew more than we all did. As an inn's owner and proprietress, she would've had her hands in every local business and heard every bit of family gossip from here to the mountains.

I chewed on my breakfast and made appropriately happy noises.

"Mmmm, this is delicious. I'm so glad we stayed here. Thank you for your hospitality, Mrs. Haségawa." I inclined my head forward, about the best I could do for a bow with a baby belly and sitting down at the table.

Haségawa brightened, surfacing from whatever thoughts she'd been having. "I'm so glad you're enjoying the food. It's always my pleasure to cook for our guests. I figure you'll be in town all day, eating festival food and walking around, and I wanted you to have a good breakfast before you left."

I looked across the table at Kayo and Akiko. Both of them shrugged at each other.

"I almost forgot about the festival," Akiko said. "What with the murder last night, I thought we might focus on that today."

"Has my love for mysteries rubbed off on you?" I teased her, and she smiled.

"Certainly not. Buuutttt..." She drew out the word. "I *am* friends with two people who love mysteries, and I don't want to see any harm come to Kayo's family, so I'm in. I'm just grateful that this murder has nothing to do with me."

Haségawa and Utako exchanged wary glances. I wanted to reassure them that Akiko was harmless, that bad things had happened to her, not the other way around, but I left it be. I was sure Akiko didn't want us to dwell on it. She wanted to move on.

"What's our next step?" I sipped again on my coffee and thanked the coffee gods for this wonderful life-giving beverage.

Utako looked to her mother, an unsaid plea for permission conveyed between the two. Her mother nodded.

"Well," Utako said, futzing with the placement of the plates on the table, "I think you should go talk to Juno's younger sister, Chisé. They're only a year apart in age, so they knew a lot of the same people. Juno got all the attention, though. I bet Chisé was the jealous sister."

"Really? I hardly knew her. I met her maybe twice?" Kayo turned her eyes to the ceiling as she thought about this. "Chisé never stood out in a crowd. She was there last night, at Imagawa Brewery. I wouldn't have recognized her if she hadn't been right there crying over her sister."

"Juno seemed to get all the talent and good looks," Utako

continued, "and Chisé was stuck with the job at the convenience store, the mousy hair, and the spindly legs."

"Utako!" Her mother's voice was aghast.

"It's okay, Mom. I was just about to say things have gotten better for Chisé this past year," Utako insisted. "She's still working at the convenience store part-time, but her looks have improved, and she's been learning about farming from one of the local co-ops. She's still pretty jealous of her sister, though." Utako's face froze in a frown. "I guess now she has nothing to be jealous of anymore." She pressed her fingers to her lips, and we paused a moment to reflect on the dead.

"Was she jealous of anything in particular? Her talents, maybe?" I asked, laying my hand on her arm.

"Jealous of everything, I suppose. Juno was the star of the yearly festival. She had agents from Tokyo driving here to see her every other month. She had a string of successful boyfriends. And most of all, Juno had the attention of their parents. You know how it is..."

She glanced at her own mother, but I got the feeling the two of them had an understanding about this issue because her mother nodded.

"Most of the elders in this town are old-fashioned, showering attention on one child who they expect to carry the family into the next generation." Haségawa put her hand to her heart. "That's not how we do things in this family, but it's how it's done elsewhere."

Yes, I had to convince my own mother I was worthy of the same recognition she gave my older brother. This was an issue I was well-aware of.

"So, now we have three possible suspects?" Kayo asked, holding up three fingers. "Detective Moto Sano, Seiji Sugimoto, the ex-boyfriend, and Chisé Takagi, sister of the deceased."

My stomach growled in response and a swift kick from the baby reminded me to get back to eating.

"That sounds like plenty of suspects for a brand-new case." Akiko returned to eating as well.

"I agree, and they're the most likely ones, too." Utako noticed we had cleaned out the rice bowl and stood up to grab it. "I have another idea for you. Chisé has a best friend she hangs out with a lot, Nahoko Sakurai. They're inseparable. She's probably the best person to talk to since the family will be in mourning today."

"Sakurai... Sakurai?" Kayo snapped her fingers. "I think I know that name."

"She's the one that helped your mom back when she was sick."

"Oh right. She's a vet, too." Kayo helped herself to more food.

"And you've heard about her sister." Utako nodded as she slid the room door open. "Nahoko is Nagisa's older sister. And I'm sure you'll be able to find Nagisa today at the festival amphitheater. She's Juno's understudy, and she'll be the one to take over at the show."

Hmmm, what a lucky break for Nagisa. I didn't say that out loud though. That would've been incredibly mean.

Kayo hummed and poured herself another cup of tea. "I suppose she'll be busy preparing for the big event. I think we'll make our way over to Seiji's house right after breakfast. Boyfriends first. Sisters and friends second."

CHAPTER
SEVEN

"**M**urder? Really, Mei? How does this always happen to you?"

I stared down at my phone as we pulled up to the house of Juno's ex-boyfriend, Seiji Sugimoto. Kayo had borrowed her father's car since he was going to stay home and avoid the brewery until the last possible moment. I was grateful for her skilled and slow driving. I wasn't sure if I could survive another ride with her father.

Yasahiro, on the other end of my texting conversation, though, was in danger of not surviving my few days away.

"It's fine," I texted back. "For once, it has nothing to do with me. Kayo seems to know all the people involved, though, so this time I just get to help."

I waited while he typed up his response and everyone opened their doors.

"Be careful."

"Always. I'll call later."

Phew. That went better than I thought it would. Yasahiro was a great husband. Not too overbearing or overprotective.

But once I really showed my pregnancy, he had become worried over everything I did. I had to reassure him that I was okay. It wasn't the worst thing in the world, and his attention was sweet. Eventually, he'd get used to it.

Mysteries were a part of my life now.

Hana, Kayo's mom, joined us for the day in all her green glory. Yesterday, it was pink. Today, her hair, her clothes, even her nails and shoes were green. Kayo had taken one look at her mother and opened the back door for her saying, "Mei rides up front."

Hana knew Seiji from the brewery where he was a consistent customer, so she thought she could gain us access to his house. I hoped so as we knocked on his front door.

The door opened, and his tired and worn-out face peeked across the threshold.

"Can I help you?" he asked. His red eyes shone in the early morning sun, and he scratched his scruffy face. "Hana? Oh, wait." He pointed at Kayo, pulling back to open the door a little wider. "You're Kayo Mitsuwara, one of the police officers from last night."

"Yes, I am." Her voice was hesitant. "Can we come in?"

My face heated as I realized Kayo was misrepresenting herself as a member of the Kubako police force, something she definitely was not. Not anymore.

I reached out to grab her arm as Seiji stepped away from the door to let us in, but I pulled my hand back before it made contact with her.

Who was I kidding? I had a conscience, but I didn't play by the rules. I stuck my nose in every single murder case the last year, and I got involved though I didn't have the qualifications to investigate anything. I wasn't a detective; I was a nosy busybody. I'm sure I gossiped as much as the Haségawas, the owners of the inn we had just come from.

Funny that a year ago, I would've lambasted anyone for being a gossip. Times changed, and I guessed, so did I.

Seiji's house was dark and cluttered. He probably hadn't opened a window or shade in the last day. Empty liquor bottles and beer cans littered the low table in his main room, and the TV was on but muted, a variety show playing where internet videos were shown and famous Japanese celebrities made comments on them.

Seiji stumbled across the tatami and sat down at the table, not offering anyone anything. Hana glanced in Seiji's kitchen and winced.

"Seiji, what happened in your kitchen?" she asked.

I caught a whiff of it, and my stomach turned.

"I was making dinner for Juno and me last night when I got the call..."

Whatever it was, it had been burnt and then decayed overnight in the warm kitchen.

Without being asked, Hana shoved up her sleeves and entered the kitchen ready for battle. Akiko shrugged and followed her in. Her strength didn't lie in investigations, anyway.

Seiji stared into space, so I asked Hana for a glass of water and brought it out to him.

"Drink some water. You're probably dehydrated." I pushed aside the beer cans and made room for the glass on the table.

"Thanks..." He peered up at me, his eyebrows pulling together. "I don't know you."

"No, you don't. But I'm a friend of Kayo's, and we're both here to help."

His stare shifted from piercing right through me to the

middle distance. It was the stare of loss, the uncomprehending stare. It was the stare that said he was on the edge of sanity.

My gut told me that this was a man who had lost someone he loved. He was afloat at sea without an anchor.

Kayo's face remained passive as she sat across from him, and I knew this part of her personality well enough. When she was with Goro, her partner and our good friend, they would play good cop, bad cop.

Today, I'd be the good cop.

"Seiji, you must be so broken up about Juno's death." I leaned forward, patted his arm, and pushed the glass of water closer to him. He ignored it.

"You knew her?" His voice was sleepy and slurred.

"No, I'm sorry. I did not. But I've only ever heard good things about her. That she was a talented actress and flute player."

"She was, she was. The very best."

Kayo opened her purse and pulled out her little notebook. "I heard through the gossip in town that the two of you had broken up, though. Was that true?"

"In, out, in, out." He waved his hand back and forth. "We were in and out of our relationship for years."

"But you were in now? Last night?" Kayo poised her pen above the paper.

"Yeah." A few tears formed, and he sniffed up and wiped them away. "Yeah. She was going to break things off with that..." He covered his mouth, and I had to lean in to hear the slew of swear words he strung together. It was actually quite impressive. "Sano. That detective. He thinks he's popular, the right match for Juno. My Juno."

I listened to the dishes being washed in the kitchen while Kayo scribbled away in her notebook.

"How long had they dated?" I asked.

"Dated?" His voice pitched lower, and he slammed his hand on the table. I squeaked as a can jumped into my lap and doused me with warm beer. I swiped it off with my hand before it could soak in. "They weren't dating."

"I have it on good authority that they were." Kayo pointed the pen at Seiji. "More than one person has told me they were together, and it was more than friends."

"Lies." Seiji's face was bright crimson. "That Sano bastard had been after her for years, ever since he moved here. He was always telling me how I was no good for her, that he was the better man. And every time Juno and I fought, she went to him."

Okay, I admitted that he went from grieving boyfriend to enraged psycho in no time flat. Angry vibes were pouring off of him like a tsunami, a madness that kept coming and coming.

And then he deflated, a balloon popped.

"Why did she go to him?" he whispered.

"It's okay," I whispered back, patting his arm.

"It's not okay. She went to him, and he killed her." He turned his pleading eyes on Kayo, and I shot her a warning glance. We were way out of our depth here. He was confiding in us like friends, and Kayo hadn't told him she wasn't on the case, yet she still planned to use this information to track down the killer. That killer could be him.

"How do we know you didn't kill her?" Kayo's straight-faced question nearly knocked Seiji over.

Seiji gasped, and his bright red face lost all its color. "Me? Kill Juno? Why would I kill her? I loved her. Look." He jumped up from the table and knocked it, dumping more beer cans and making more of a mess. I scooted away just in time.

Hana and Akiko finished up in the kitchen and poked

their heads out of the doorway, joining us to watch Seiji enter his bedroom and toss stuff around.

"Here!" He barreled out of the bedroom and thrust a box at Kayo. Her throat bobbed as she held the ring box. "Juno picked that out herself. Go ahead and call the number on the receipt. They saw her there, saw us there, picking out this ring. We were going to be married. Why would I kill someone I wanted to spend the rest of my life with?"

Good question. I rubbed the tip of my thumb against my own ring, one Yasahiro had picked out with the help of Akiko. Seiji never got to put the ring on Juno's finger.

Kayo opened the box and looked at the engagement ring. It was the real deal. Nothing huge and extravagant, but it was tasteful and pretty.

I glanced over at the table we had just sat at. Seiji had run the gamut of emotions in the twenty minutes we'd spoken. From sadness to violence to grief, I could see him being so stricken he'd kill someone.

Kayo pulled her phone from her pocket, snapped a photo of the receipt, and handed everything back to Seiji. I had no doubt that she'd follow up with the store and make sure Juno had been there.

Seiji slumped against the wall, his arm slack with the ring box clutched in his hand.

Motive and opportunity, right? It was time to establish his alibi for the day, though with poison, there was a window in which she could have ingested it.

"Can you tell us more about what you did yesterday?" I asked. Outside, the sounds of gravel crunching grew louder, and a car rumbled up to the house. Hana and Akiko went to the front door.

"I worked in the morning from home," he said, waving to

his desk across the room and the quiet laptop sitting on it. "Then I met Juno for lunch at the festival."

I remembered him meeting her there after she had purchased her salad and had spoken to Hana.

"We spent a few hours together, and then she said she had to meet up with someone. It was business, and I didn't ask who." His jaw tightened. "I had come to trust her and not question her every move. We were going to be married..." He sank even more into the wall.

Akiko rushed up next to me and leaned into my ear. "The police are here."

I swallowed, and my forehead began to sweat.

"I think we'll get going now. We don't want to bother you even more," I began, but a rapping at the door stopped me.

Kayo flipped her notebook closed and stashed it in her purse. If she was nervous at all, she didn't betray her feelings to anyone.

"We're so sorry for your loss. Truly," she said, squeezing Seiji's arm. "Hopefully talking it through helped you —"

"Seiji Sugimoto, it's Detective Ichikawa with the Kubako Police Department." The voice was unfamiliar, but it carried through the door. "Open the door."

There was no saying "no" to this request, it was clear.

Seiji hung his head and didn't move.

"I'll open the door," Hana said, approaching the front, and when Seiji didn't stop her, we all nodded.

I turned to get a view of the front, and through the opening door, I could see two squad cars and a black sedan parked outside. On the porch, a man and woman, both dressed in suits, waited with two other male police officers in uniform. They had come in strength. Other police officers may be out circling the house to make sure Seiji didn't make a run for it.

But he wasn't going anywhere. Seiji was a puppet whose strings had been cut. He could barely hold himself upright. Kayo slipped her hand under his armpit and urged him to walk forward.

"Kayo Mitsuwara? You're the last person we expected to see here," said the female detective. They bowed to each other.

Hana held her hand to her chest. "Well, after what happened last night, I felt compelled to check on Seiji, and it's a good thing I did. He's a mess, and so was his kitchen." She gestured both to Seiji and the rubber gloves still in her hand.

"I see," the detective said. "That certainly is kind of you all to stop by."

"We were worried," Kayo said. "That's all. Kubako residents look out for each other."

The male detective, probably Ichikawa, coolly looked us over, but his eyes settled on Kayo.

"Kayo, I didn't expect to see you here." His tone of voice was skeptical and hard as frost. I tried not to shrink or move in any kind of submissive way. I knew men like this, men who looked for any sort of weakness and exploited it.

Kayo smiled, and I wanted to smirk at how easily she shrugged off Ichikawa's frosty greeting.

Keep your lips still, Mei.

"I'm in town for a visit, and on day one, someone is murdered in my parents' brewery. It wasn't the greeting I was expecting."

Ichikawa's ice-cold smile lowered a few degrees.

"We only roll out the red carpet for the real celebrities."

Kayo raised her eyebrows but didn't respond.

"We're here to bring Seiji Sugimoto into the station for questioning. You weren't, perhaps, coaching my witness, were you? You have no jurisdiction here." He folded his arms across his chest and grew at least two sizes. "Isn't Chikata some little backwater town in Fukushima prefecture?"

"Saitama," I said, my defenses perking up. "And if forty minutes from Tokyo is backwater, then I have no idea where this town is."

His face didn't change one bit. But Akiko smiled, stopped a giggle, and looked at her feet.

Seiji didn't even protest. He looked at Kayo, and she nodded to him as she helped him forward and into the hands of the female detective. They made their way slowly out the door to the officers waiting on the porch.

"I assume you're staying with your parents?" Ichikawa unfolded his arms and retrieved his phone from the front pocket of his jacket.

"No. Haségawa Ryokan," Kayo said, sighing. "Why do you care?"

He punched a note into his phone, his massive thumbs tapping away at the screen. "Because if I find out you've been sticking your nose in my investigation, I'll know where to find you." He put his phone away and pointed at Kayo. "Don't get involved."

When the door closed, Kayo rolled her eyes, but her shoulders were up around her ears. Ichikawa had intimidated her.

"I always hated him," she said, as she glanced around Seiji's main room. "Let's clean this up and go."

As Akiko and Hana picked up the empty beer cans, I thought about the life Kayo had here before moving to Chikata. Ichikawa, the cold and unfeeling lead detective. Sano, a hothead detective who took credit for Kayo's work. Kayo's wacky family. And finally, an ex-boyfriend she couldn't get away from.

No wonder she moved.

CHAPTER
EIGHT

The crowd gasped and cheered as the two-story-tall float spun and dancers swirled around it. Akiko, Kayo, Hana, and I laughed and shouted, waving to the kids who proudly walked with their parents in the parade, and the morning's somber events faded a bit. It was hard to have fun when murder was on my mind.

The Fall Festival was in full swing on this bright and sunny Saturday morning. Kubako was a much bigger town than Chikata, at least three times the size, so though I had expected to see a lot of long faces about Juno's death, the scene was quite the opposite. People along the main street talked and laughed, all the food stalls set up along the two side streets were teeming with customers, and the parade started right on time. Juno may have been a star, but the town's plans went on without her.

"Anyone else find it weird that no one is talking about Juno's death?" I asked, clapping and smiling at the dance troupe following another giant float of a dragon.

"I'm not surprised," Akiko said, waving to a kid riding on

her father's shoulders. "This is a big town. The world doesn't stop just because one person dies."

"Yeah, you're right."

Back in Chikata, everything in town had kept on running when Akiko's father had died. We grieved for him, but only a handful of us went to the funeral. Even if Juno had been a movie star, it's doubtful the town would've postponed the festival. Everyone here got on with their lives.

"Oh, look, the musicians' float is coming up!" Hana pointed and smiled at the long float being pulled by a truck. On the traveling platform, taiko drummers banged away a fast rhythm while dancing. Behind them, two *shamisen* players strummed and a flute player trilled a tune between them. She was young, maybe in her mid-twenties, with long, straight jet-black hair and a pale oval face. Was this Juno's replacement? I was drawn into her performance immediately. The music, hitting high notes and descending in a perfect scale, shot up my back and raised the hairs on my arm. She was amazing.

"That must be her, Nagisa, Juno's understudy," Kayo said in my ear. "Hard to believe she was second chair for so long."

It was hard to believe. Nagisa moved like liquid, possessed by the music. If she didn't do this professionally, I would be sorely disappointed in her. Her music should be heard far and wide. I tore my eyes from the float as it slid past us and scanned the crowd. Everyone else was just as captivated as I was.

"She's got a whole lot of talent. I'm impressed." I had to catch my breath, and for once, my baby was also enthralled enough to sit still in my belly. She was just as quiet as I was.

"I think I need a new charm from the temple," Hana said, opening her bag and digging around inside. "I lost mine a few days ago, and I don't want to be without one for long."

Charms were important. My own *omamori* that I bought from Inari Fushimi Shrine in Kyoto three years ago sat in my wallet. The paper printed with a blessing and the tiny fox charm made of wood helped bring me good fortune in both business and at home. I tried not to leave home without it. I didn't want to be without its protective benefits for even a moment.

"Let's follow the musicians' float to the end of the route," Kayo said, jerking her chin in the direction toward the main temple's gate. "If we follow now, we'll get out of the crush of people, and we can get food when we're done."

I took Akiko's hand and let her clear a path in front of us. With someone directing me along, I had less of a chance of being crushed. People always got out of Akiko's way, and she was protective of my pregnancy as much as anyone I was related to. She said "excuse me" over and over, plowing her way through and around clumps of people.

We made it all the way to the temple and into the crowd before I heard the sirens in the distance. It was one of those things, after living in Tokyo for so long, I hardly ever paid attention to sirens unless they were on top of me. But in a new town, they caught my ear. Up on my tip toes, I looked left and right to see if we were in the way of an ambulance. But all I saw was a cop car crawling to the side streets.

"Look," Akiko said in my ear. "Over there."

I followed her gesture to the far side of the gravel yard we were standing in and saw the flutist, Nagisa, amid a group of people. She was smiling and bowing, flushed with the praise people were laying on her. Another young woman stood next to her, smiling just as widely, her hand on Nagisa's shoulder. They were obviously sisters.

"Think those two are sisters?" Akiko asked, and Kayo slid into our conversation looking at them as well.

"They are. That's Nahoko, Nagisa's older sister, one of the veterinarians in town."

The sounds of the siren grew louder again, and this time it caught Kayo's attention too.

"What's going on?" She turned and made towards the exit, out the way we just came in. "Have you seen my mom?"

Huh. Hana was gone. Had she followed us into the temple? I thought she had.

I grabbed onto Akiko's bag as she snaked through the crowd right behind Kayo. How had I not noticed Hana's absence? She was an adult though. She probably saw someone she knew and got pulled into a conversation.

"Kayo!" The voice was authoritative and stopped Kayo in her tracks. She twitched and grimaced as the man approaching her shouted her name again in anger. Well, that was rude.

Oh, it was Detective Sano. I guessed I shouldn't have been surprised.

"What's this I hear about you questioning my witness this morning?" Sano stepped right into Kayo's personal space, and this time she couldn't help but step back... into Akiko who bumped into me.

"Hey, watch it!" I admonished him. He scoffed at me.

Even ruder.

"Your witness?" Kayo recovered, raising her chin. "More like Ichikawa's witness. You don't get to participate in a murder investigation if you're one of the suspects."

"Me? A suspect?" He smiled and chuckled. "You've lost your mind in that little unknown town you've moved to."

"Listen here," I said, jostling forward and poking him in the chest. "The next person that insults my hometown is going to get a knee right in the groin." He raised his hands in surrender, but his cocky smile boiled my insides, and red tinted everything around me. "Look here, idiot. I'm on vacation." I lowered my voice. "Don't test a pregnant woman. I have hormones that could beat you senseless."

His smile faded, and Akiko whistled low.

The red in my vision clung to the edges, and I snapped back to the situation at hand. My hormones had had just about enough of his nonsense.

"Okay, okay," he said, his manner changing and backing down. I had to remember this for later, for the next time some aggressive man tried to push me around. I had an angry side, and I should use it more often.

"We visited Sugimoto because my mother was worried about him. He had every right to speak with us, if he wanted to, and he did." Kayo waggled her head at Sano, her shoulders bopping along with it. "He was going to marry Juno. They had a ring and everything. What were you doing trying to poach someone else's fiancée? Can't you leave well enough alone?"

Sano's jaw tightened. "I... It's none of your business. What should be your business is figuring out why your family would poison the saké that killed her."

"My family? Poison Juno? You must be mad. And in fact, I'm making it my business. All of it."

Sano threw his head back and laughed. "Mad? Your family is crazy. Total lunatics, all of them. Especially your father. Have you seen him drive? Half the time he's running around town in full-on samurai armor acting like it's the 1600s. Your mother dresses every color of the rainbow. Your sister is a lesbian who believes in mermaids. And your older brother spent five years living as a monk in Tibet."

It was as if the closet burst open and all the dusty skeletons in the world fell out and littered the ground. Kayo's hand curled into a ball, and I slid my hand over it to hold it still.

In the year we had known each other, Kayo had rarely spoken about her family. Little comments here and there about her family doing well or busy, and she had returned home for New Year's Day as well. But details? They had been few and far between. Maybe she'd finally felt comfortable in her friendships with Akiko and me, enough to throw us into the deep end with her family? I didn't know.

I didn't care.

She was one of my closest friends, and she didn't deserve this kind of treatment.

I slid myself in front of Kayo. There wasn't much room there for all of me and my pregnant belly, but it forced Sano to step away. "Just because her family is eccentric doesn't mean they're psychotic. And you have no actual proof the saké was poisoned. Juno could've been poisoned by anything."

"She *was* poisoned, though, and she died at *your* brewery." He jabbed his index finger past me to Kayo.

"Wait —" I started.

"The toxicology report came back?" Kayo interrupted from behind me.

Sano's eyes widened, and his face lost a few shades of angry red.

"She was definitely poisoned?" I asked. "It wasn't death by natural causes?"

I looked over at Akiko who had been silent until now, always the observer. She shrugged. "Called it."

I let this news brew in the back of my head. Juno was definitely murdered in the Imagawa Brewery... or maybe the place of the murder didn't matter at all.

"What was the poison?" Kayo's voice was the hard tone she used at work.

I didn't think Sano would answer. "Hemlock," he blurted out and then deflated. He couldn't hold it together to defy us any longer. I took that as a good sign. "They didn't find any ingested hemlock, though."

Kayo paused, her eyes flitting left and right. "If I remember correctly, hemlock poisoning can occur anywhere from thirty minutes to several hours after being eaten. But if there was no plant matter in her stomach, then who knows how it got in her system or how strong it was."

"Sounds like the poisoning could've happened anywhere before she arrived at the brewery," I pointed out. "That means there's even less of a chance the saké poisoned her. Besides, if that had happened, other people would've gotten sick too.

Sano ran his hand through his hair and sighed. "I'm not going to have you people interfering with my investigation."

"*Your* investigation?" Kayo's voice rose.

"No way," Akiko said, butting in. "You're a suspect now."

"She's right." I nodded at Akiko, proud of her for getting involved.

"Me? A suspect?" Sano stepped away, holding his hands palms out.

Akiko stepped towards him. "Maybe you poisoned Juno yourself? Maybe you were angry with her for choosing Seiji over you? And with your chance to date the star of the town gone, you couldn't let anyone else have her."

We were drawing a crowd now. Several people gathered around us, whispering behind raised hands. One younger man pulled his phone out of his pocket and filmed us. Sano finally realized where he was and what was going on as he took another step back and the crowd moved to accommodate him.

"Oi!" he yelled at the crowd. "Move along."

A few people grumbled and shuffled out of the way, but someone pointed past us to thundering feet running up the street.

Five police officers were heading straight for us.

"Sano!" The man in the lead ran up to Sano and huffed to catch his breath. "Come quickly. It's Kobayashi. We think she's been poisoned."

CHAPTER
NINE

Through the crush of people at the end of the parade, the street opened up, and we hustled towards the flashing lights of the police car. Kayo and the police were in the lead, and Akiko and I brought up the rear a lot slower. There's only so much hustling I can do when I'm waddling like a duck.

Around the corner to the food stalls, we ran right into Hana talking to another woman, both turned towards the chaos down the street. It was Manari Haségawa, the owner of the inn we were staying at.

"What's going on? Was someone really poisoned again?" Akiko asked as an ambulance rounded the corner and parked next to the police car.

"I left Utako back at the ryokan so I could come out to get us food from the festival." Haségawa's face was ashen as she flung out her arm in the direction of the chaos. "I stopped to speak to some of the police officers I know. Just some friendly chit-chat. And one of the younger officers went into convulsions and fell over. A woman named Kobayashi."

Hana pressed her green-nailed fingers to her lips. Her face had taken on a green tinge along with everything she was wearing. "Oh. That's the woman who helped Seiji out of his house this morning."

"Really?" I asked, remembering the younger woman in a suit who accompanied Ichikawa. "That seems... suspicious."

"Very," Hana agreed.

We waited until the emergency rescue crews had loaded the young woman onto a stretcher and wheeled her into the ambulance before approaching the scene. In the time it took for Kobayashi to be whisked away, the rest of the police had cordoned off the area. Police officers held out their arms and kept the crowd back while other officers stood around the crime scene.

And what a crime scene it was. Kubako must have had quite a large police force because there were at least ten off-duty police officers, now displaying their badges on their belts or hanging off collars, milling about the "lunch table" they had arranged in a quiet patch of a private garden just off the main street. As was typical of many street fairs in Japan, people were expected to stand at the food stalls and wolf down their snack before they moved on, or they had to shoot off to other areas to find seating or an open space to eat.

Since this was their town, the officers knew where to go to find a spot to eat. The old man who owned the house's garden stood at the back entrance to his home, his eyes worried.

"I wasn't even out here," I could hear him saying to an on-duty officer. "I never have a problem sharing my garden with the police. What a wretched thing to happen."

And there was no way this man was ever sharing his garden again, I could tell you that. He looked ready to burn the whole place down and start over again. At the very least, he'd get someone out here to say prayers over his house and garden to rid it of the bad juju it had just gained.

"This is a nightmare," Sano said, coming up next to us. He had just spoken with the neighbor across the street.

"Sir," one officer called out, and Ichikawa stood up from examining the crime scene to face Sano. Their eyes locked, and for a second, I swore I saw flames coming from Ichikawa's ears. We backed away from the garden gate as Ichikawa took three long steps and jumped Sano.

I screamed and tripped backwards into Hana and Akiko. They yelped as I trampled on Hana's foot and elbowed Akiko in the chest. We knocked over a potted plant, and I landed on my butt.

The fight was off to a raucous start. Ichikawa and Sano were a tangle of limbs, hair, and dirt as they pummeled one another. *Crush, crunch.* Oooh. That had to hurt. Other officers stood around with their eyes wide and mouths open. Ichikawa rolled Sano over, pinning him to the ground, and finally, another officer came forward to help him.

Either they had all been shocked to see these two men beating each other up, or they had been waiting to see who won.

I couldn't blame them for holding back. That was a lot of pent-up aggression.

Sano struggled to get loose, but Ichikawa held him still.

"Two women dead in two days, and you're the only connection between them."

Sano seethed beneath Ichikawa, and Ichikawa raised his hand to the officers behind him. "Cuffs," he demanded.

"I didn't do it. I didn't poison them!" Blood poured from Sano's nose as he shouted.

"Don't tell me you hadn't been dating Kobayashi, right

under my nose. You think I didn't see it? You think I'm blind?" He snapped the cuffs on Sano's wrists. "I know she dumped you for someone else. You must have been shocked to find all the women in your life looking to get rid of you."

I cringed away from the words, not used to being privy to the intimate details of a stranger's life. Kayo watched the two of them, utterly rapt, caught up in the drama. She had worked with them both in the past. This must have been a trip for her.

She blinked and came back to the present, slipping around Sano and Ichikawa to help pick me off the ground.

"You okay?" she asked, as I came to my feet.

"Yeah. I'm fine." We both turned around and checked out Akiko and Hana. They were unscathed if a little dirty from colliding with the potted plant.

Ichikawa hauled Sano off the ground, both of them bloody and battered.

Was this it? Was the case solved this quickly? It felt too easy, too staged. And I doubted that anyone who was a detective would be this sloppy in committing two murders back to back. That is if Kobayashi didn't live to tell us what happened.

I rested my hands on my belly eager to feel the baby move, and she swirled around, practically on command. Phew. So far I'd had a routine pregnancy, and I didn't want something as mundane as a police catfight to ruin it.

I chuckled as I watched Ichikawa push Sano into a patrol car.

"What's so funny?" Kayo asked, a subtle smile crossing her lips.

"Oh, you know. My life. I can't escape drama lately."

"Yeah, I feel the same way." She folded her arms across her chest and frowned as the car pulled away.

"Are you thinking what I'm thinking?" I whispered, trying

not to call attention to our presence. The leftover officers stood in clumps, their voices low, and everyone ignored the crime scene. They may have been waiting for forensics to show up.

"That Sano is a jerk and got what was coming to him?"

"Besides that."

"If you're thinking they're still after the wrong guy, then I agree with you." Kayo let her arms loose at her side. "But what do I know, right? I haven't been on active duty here in over two years. Sano could be a great guy, and Seiji could be a killer in disguise. I could be totally wrong."

Or she could be right and someone was still out there trying to kill more people.

"Let's..." Kayo jerked her head in the direction of the crime scene.

Sure. Why not? I doubted anyone would arrest us.

Hana had backed off and was talking to Haségawa again, farther away from the garden, and Akiko seemed eager, poised on the tips of her toes.

"You talk to the officers, and I'll sneak some photos," she said. I smiled at her sudden change of heart about police investigations. Maybe she was ready to move on.

As we entered the garden, almost everyone ignored us. They were all too busy gossiping about the fight to secure the area.

Kayo walked up to the clump of officers closest to the lunch area.

"Kayo!" Several smiled and bowed or offered hands for shaking. She may not have had a good relationship with Ichikawa or Sano, but it appeared she still had friends in the lower ranks. These four seemed like an amiable bunch.

"Hey guys, it's great to see you, though not so much under present circumstances."

"Can you believe that?" one guy asked.

"I've never seen Ichikawa take air. It was like he was possessed by a dragon."

"I didn't know he could fight. Think he's taken jiu-jitsu?"

"We all take jiu-jitsu, moron."

"Yeah, but not in a while."

"We were all just having lunch and boom. She was convulsing on the ground."

"I wonder if they'll fire Sano. I hope so."

"Looking for a promotion?"

"As if you aren't."

My head bounced back and forth listening to the four of them bandy about barbs and comments on the situation. Small town, big city — it didn't matter. Everyone dealt with workplace gossip and competition.

"So, what do you think? Did he do it?" Kayo rocked back on her heels. I did my best not to look past the cops to the discarded lunches where Akiko was snapping photos and crouching down to examine food left behind.

"Sano? Kill Juno Takagi and Kobayashi?" The only female cop in the group scoffed. She seemed familiar. "Of course he did. You didn't hear what happened last year."

"What?" I stepped a little closer, and two of the guys looked confused wondering who I was. "What happened?"

"It was at the year-end *nomikai*," the female officer said, and two of the guys rolled their eyes. I hadn't been to a nomikai, a work drinking party, in a long time, especially not a year-end drinking party which usually got sloppy and overly sentimental. "Aw, come on." She slapped one guy's arm. "It was more than could be overlooked."

"Yes, yes," he said, still rolling his eyes.

Another thing about nomikai was that, even if you got

sloppy drunk and did something stupid, all would be forgiven and forgotten the next day. Unless someone held a grudge that is.

"Sano got so drunk, he plastered himself all over one of the admins, a sweet girl, couldn't have been older than twenty-one. Then he tripped, grabbed her skirt, and pulled it right off."

Kayo gasped. "No."

"Yes."

"What happened?"

"She complained to her boss the next day, and then Sano started a campaign against her to get her fired," she continued. One officer listened to her while the other took out his phone and scrolled through whatever was on the screen. "Sabotaged her reports. Killed her plant on her desk. Left rotting food in her bag. Little, petty stuff, but it was enough for her to quit."

"Forensics is on the way." The other officer put his phone away and turned around to view the crime scene. I caught my breath, but Akiko was nowhere in sight. Everything looked normal.

Well, as normal as a crime scene gets. At least it wasn't all bloody.

"I warned Kobayashi not to get involved with him, but she did it anyway." The female officer clicked her tongue and shook her head. "But it didn't last long. She broke up with him, and he got even more bitter and surly at work. It was no fun for anyone."

"When was that?" Kayo asked as the forensics van pulled up.

"Only three weeks ago. He went right out and started pursuing Juno Takagi practically the next day. Everyone thought he was crazy to go after the most popular woman in town, especially since she was back on again with her ex-boyfriend. But she seemed to tolerate it."

"Tolerate?" A pit of dread grew in my stomach.

"At best." She turned away to join the others, walked backwards, and said, "He was a police officer bent on dating her. I got the feeling she was intimidated by him. Ask her sister. She was there, drinking with them last night, and I questioned her just after it happened. I think you may have met her. What's her name?" She snapped her fingers. "Right. Chisé."

Now I could place this officer! She was the one who pulled Juno's sister aside to question her last night. Everything in the previous eighteen hours was a blur, and I was asleep for some of it.

We edged past the crime scene and met Akiko and Hana out on the sidewalk.

"I guess this is good news for the brewery, Mom. No one here was drinking saké."

"Good news for sure. Bad for many others," Hana mumbled, keeping her voice low. "Let's return to the house for lunch. I don't trust eating at the festival anymore. I'll make tonkatsu!"

No fair food, but I smiled at the thought of fried pork cutlets for lunch. I could be okay with that.

CHAPTER
TEN

This was better than sitting on a hard park bench for lunch. Hana set up a cushiony spot for me at the *kotatsu*, the heated table, and I snuggled down into the warmth as I nibbled on my pork cutlet, cabbage, and rice.

"Your father will be so happy to hear that the brewery's name will be cleared at the end of this mess. The rumors will spread for some time, but he's already saying the loyal customers came by today for drinks with their lunches." Hana dipped her green head to take a bite of her cutlet and then a sip of saké. I was a wee bit jealous of everyone having hot saké with their meal today.

Kayo nodded as she sat back from her empty plate. "I wish there was more I could do. I feel lost not being able to help."

Hana covered Kayo's hand with her own, and the gesture warmed my heart. "You've already done a lot, more than most people could in this situation. I know I've never said much about you becoming a police officer, but I'm proud of the way you've handled yourself."

Kayo's cheeks reddened, and she looked away, but she

grasped her mother's fingers in her own. I smiled at Akiko, and she returned it. I finally felt better about the whole situation.

But not enough to stop investigating.

"So does this mean we're giving up on the murder case?" I asked, finishing off the last bit of pork cutlet. Tonkatsu was one of my favorite meals. Even with a smaller stomach now that my baby had taken up that space, I still could always finish a cutlet... and the sauce on top of it. I dumped a substantial portion of my rice from my bowl onto the plate to capture the remaining sauce and chopped cabbage.

"We got involved to make sure Dad's brewery was cleared of any wrongdoing. And I think we're in the clear now, right?"

"Sure," I said, and Akiko's head bopped right along with mine. "But..."

"We're kind of already involved now, aren't we? And you didn't see what I saw in the photos I took today."

Akiko's smile was small and devious, something I hadn't seen in a long time. She'd spent the last year in mourning, angry and alone. I was glad to see she was back to her old self if even for a small amount of time. Funny, it was a murder that got her to that dark place and another that brought her out.

Life is strange.

"Okay, now I'm interested." Kayo held her hand out. "Let's see those photos."

Akiko swiped on her phone and navigated to her photo album before handing over the phone. Kayo narrowed her eyes as she examined every photo. She hummed, zooming into some of them, chewing on her lip, and swiping to the next one.

After a few minutes, my knee started to bounce. "Come on and finish up. I want to see." I wiggled my fingers in her direction.

"Okay, okay." She laughed and handed over the phone. "You tell me if you see what I see."

I started with the overall photo of the lunch scene. On the small tables in the center of the garden, several discarded lunches awaited consumption. Chicken skewers, rice, and a Coke. Takoyaki and green tea. Fried noodles with pork and a bottle of water. Mixed seafood salad, a rice ball, and a cup of coffee.

Hmmm, I saw nothing out of the ordinary here. This was all festival food, festival food I loved, and suddenly, I was hungry again looking at it. Damn those pregnancy hormones. They gave me no peace!

I swiped to the next photo, and it was the same food from a different perspective. This time I saw a few plastic bags also lying under the tables. They were bunched up, probably to be recycled, like many people do. Several photos later, I still had no idea what I was missing. I zoomed in and looked around, but nope. No clue.

"I give up. I'm not sure what I'm supposed to see here."

After a moment of locking eyes with Kayo, Akiko smiled and scooted over next to me. She pointed to each lunch. "One, two, three, four. Four lunches."

The puzzle made sense.

"Ah! When we arrived, we talked to the four officers who were having lunch with Kobayashi. So if there are four lunches here, and they all belonged to the four officers, where was Kobayashi's lunch? Or maybe, someone else wasn't eating? Hmmmm."

"Hmmm is right. Maybe she ate before she came and met up with everyone? Maybe that's when she was poisoned." Kayo crossed her arms and lowered herself further under the kotatsu looking for warmth and possibly a nap. She closed her eyes for a millisecond before her head snapped back up, and she picked up her phone from the table. Hana, sensing this would be a long call, got up from the table and picked up everyone's plates.

"Hi, may I speak to Officer Joy Senju... Thank you." Kayo waited while she picked at her cuticles. "Joy, hi! It's Kayo Mitsuwara... Yes, it was good to see you today as well, especially under the circumstances. How is Kobayashi? ... Oh, oh no. I'm sorry to hear this. Damn."

Kayo looked up and made a slashing motion across her neck.

Kobayashi was dead. Two murders in less than twenty-four hours.

"I'll send my condolences to her family... I know. It's tragic. It really is... Hey, I have a few questions for you, if you don't mind. At lunch today, did you all eat with Kobayashi? ... Right. But did she eat right in front of you? ... I see. She ate before she showed up with Sano? Huh. Why was she with Sano? ... He was trying to convince her he wasn't involved in Takagi's death? Well, that's looking less likely now, isn't it? Any idea what she had to eat? No? Okay... One more thing, can I get the address for the Takagi family? My mom and I want to drop by and see if they need anything. Sure." Kayo scrambled to the side and grabbed a pen and paper from a low table where her father's computer sat. "Go ahead." She scribbled down the address. "Thanks, Joy..." Kayo laughed. "No, I'm not returning any day soon, but that's sweet. Thank you. Talk to you soon."

She hung up and smiled down at her phone.

"She was always one of the nicer ones. Her mother is Filipino, hence the non-Japanese name. Anyway, I knew I could count on her to tell me what's going on."

"Sano was involved in this poisoning too?" I asked.

"It looks like it, or someone's doing a great job of framing him for the job." Kayo rubbed her face. "I don't know about this. I can't help but think someone has an agenda, and if we get in the way, we'll be taken down too. It seems dangerous to stick our nose in this when we don't even have any jurisdiction here."

"I think we can avoid poison pretty easily," Akiko said, shrugging.

"In my experience, those willing to kill by poison will kill by other means too. That doesn't mean we're safe," Kayo pointed out, and I had to nod in agreement. Akiko had direct experience with this too. She frowned as she drummed her fingers on the table.

Maybe it *was* dangerous to get involved in something like this, but we were also outsiders, and I doubted we were high on the list to become victims. The murderer had a list he or she was working with. This person was calculating and betting on a particular outcome, I could feel it.

If we were going to do this, we needed to figure out their motive. We had their method, poisoning, down, but not how or why. It was time to get back to the core of solving mysteries.

"Motive, method, and opportunity," I said, and Akiko's eyes brightened while Kayo smiled. "I've made my choice. I'm in."

"Me too." Akiko raised her hand.

"Me too!" Hana called out from the kitchen.

We all chuckled.

"Great. Let's get started with our suspects."

CHAPTER
ELEVEN

"We're going to solve this crime in the next..." Kayo glanced at her phone. "Six hours. Before the fireworks at 20:00."

"We are?" I asked, looking at my phone. It was almost 14:00, and my after-lunch nap time was approaching. But I took one look at Kayo and knew an afternoon nap was off the table. Her cheeks shined, and her eyes sparkled with excitement. What was it about this case that had so enthralled her?

"Ah!" I raised my finger in the air. "Goro's not here to hold you back on this one, right?"

"Well..." She dragged out the word and raised her eyes to the ceiling.

Her partner back home was also a good friend, Goro Hokichi, and he outranked her on most of the cases they worked together. I'm sure she wasn't bitter about it or anything. Goro had plenty of knowledge to impart to Kayo, and he was always supportive. But without him here to take the lead, it was all up to Kayo for once.

"It's okay," I said, giving her a warm smile. "I know how hard you work. Sure. Let's solve this case before the fireworks."

"Great!" Kayo jumped up from her seat. "Be right back."

She ran down the hall to her mother's craft room and returned with a dry erase board and marker. Akiko and I both chuckled while Kayo leaned the dry erase board against the wall and knelt beside it.

"What?" She laughed and shrugged. "This is what I always do. Remember the big board I put together on Amanda Cheung?"

I swallowed as I remembered the giant evidence board at the station when the Chikata police were working on Yasahiro's ex-girlfriend's case.

"How could I forget?" My voice had lost its warmth, and both Kayo and Akiko froze in place.

"Sorry," Kayo whispered and cleared her throat. "Let's get to business."

I tried to let the memories of that awful time fade away as Kayo wrote on the board. She put "Juno Takagi" up at the top and "Poisoned - Hemlock" under that and then started on her suspects.

"The first suspect is Seiji Sugimoto. Means, motive, and opportunity?" she asked, and Akiko and I looked at each other, at a loss for words.

Then I piped up. "Well, everyone had the means to poison Juno, no? Hemlock grows wild around here, I think."

I took out my phone and did a quick Google search.

"Yeah, see here? Hemlock grows wild in Mie Prefecture. There are close-up photos of it and everything." I stared down at my phone. The damned internet made it easy for anyone to be a murderer these days. No more trudging off to the library to research the best way to poison someone or get rid of a dead body. You could do that all online now.

How convenient.

Kayo twirled the dry erase marker in her fingers. "Okay, then. Everyone had means. Let's concentrate on opportunity. He had the opportunity to poison Juno since he was with her all afternoon. We saw her leave the festival food stalls with him, and then he said they had been together at the festival until she left to meet up with Sano."

"Right," I said, warming up. "We saw her leave the same food stall line your mother was in."

"What was I in?" Hana returned to the room to sit and pay attention. "Hey, isn't that my dry erase board?"

"You weren't using it." Kayo waved her off, her mind devoted to the information at hand. She scribbled Seiji's name on the board and wrote, "With her in the afternoon."

"Motive is sketchier." Akiko sat forward, getting into the mix. "He seemed upset about Juno dating someone else, but if he knew they were going to be married, he wouldn't worry about that long term. And! Let's not forget he had nothing to do with Kobayashi."

"Yes! I believe he's still in a holding cell at the station." Kayo hummed. "Unless he's working with an accomplice?"

I shrugged, realizing this would become complicated if we considered accomplices. "I suppose it could happen."

"Let's assume not for right now. Most murderers work alone otherwise they worry about being found out." Kayo wrote, "Motive - Juno seeing someone else," under Seiji's name.

"Okay, onto Detective Moto Sano," she said, scribbling away. "He had plenty of opportunity for both Juno and Kobayashi. Slip the poison into her snacks or saké at the brewery and then destroy the evidence because he's a police officer. Same with Kobayashi."

"And motive," I continued. "He was upset over being spurned by two lovers? I don't really know him though he comes across as a jerk."

"He is," Kayo said, adding more information to the board. "Do I think he's a murderer, though?"

We all sat quietly, staring at the board. These two men were the prime suspects, but there were more.

"Maybe. Maybe not." Kayo tilted her head side-to-side. "Who's next?"

"Chisé Takagi," I pointed out. "Juno's younger sister."

"The *jealous* younger sister," Akiko stressed. "Her older sister steals the show all the time, leaving her out of the familial attention. You said it." She points at Kayo. "Your friend, Joy, said it. Utako said it. I bet Juno even stood to inherit the house and land."

"I'll say it too." Hana raised her hand, and I smiled at the schoolgirl-like quality she took on. All dressed in one color she did look a lot younger. Maybe that was the point. "I spend a lot of time at the brewery helping out Dad. I've seen them bicker when they've been there together."

Kayo hummed, thinking about this.

"But, in all fairness, I also saw them laugh and be kind to each other too." Hana flipped her hand out to the side. "What can I say, but 'sisters, you know?'"

"I do," Kayo responded, and I wondered how well she got along with her sister, the one Sano said was a lesbian who believed in mermaids. "Still, she goes up on the board." Kayo wrote "Chisé Takagi" up on the board. "Motive, she was jealous of her older sister and wanted her gone. And she stood to gain financially if Juno was gone."

I cringed. "I hate it when money is the main motive. It just feels wrong to kill someone for money."

"That's because you have a conscience. There may be another motive we're missing. We'll have to dig."

My insides squirmed, and this time it wasn't the baby. She was sleeping off my food coma from lunch with little bubbles of movement every now and then. I'd had thought this awful thought before, and I pushed it down again.

But it popped up like a rubber duck in the bath.

"What about...?" I bit my lip and stopped.

"What about what, Mei?" Kayo asked, scrolling through something on her phone.

I forced it out. "Nagisa. The flute player."

"What about her?" Kayo lifted her head from her phone.

I pulled up the blanket Hana had given me, hoping for more warmth from the kotatsu. A chill had settled into my lower back, a chill I felt was Juno, sitting and waiting for me to say more. I never did like ghosts.

"Well, she was terrific, right?" Everyone nodded. "It was like she was meant to be there on that float. The music possessed her, and the crowd was enraptured. I bet tonight, at the festival performance, she'll be even more impressive."

Kayo stared at me.

"Imagine being in Nagisa's shoes. She's amazing and knows it. But she'll never get to be in the spotlight with Juno always around."

"So she kills her competition to get the lead in the play?" Akiko's eyebrows practically lifted off from her forehead.

I shrugged. "It's not something I would do, or you, or anyone we know. But my guess is that when you're that passionate about your work, when you're that good, you'd do anything to be able to fulfill your desire to perform."

Hana nodded. "I understand this drive. Not enough to kill, of course. But I would move or sell all my belongings or go without food to continue my fashion design. It's that important to me."

Kayo looked at her mother for a long moment before she sighed, turned to the board, and added Nagisa Sakurai to the list. Under her name, she wrote, "Motive - to play in the main performance. Opportunity - ??"

"There are far too many questions here and not enough answers." Kayo snapped the top back on the dry erase marker and set it on the table. "Did I really say we'd solve this mystery in six hours?"

"You did indeed," I reminded her.

Kayo's phone buzzed, and she picked it up to look at it. "Joy's been texting me. I always liked her. She's a good person. Very reliable. She says the preliminary reports on Kobayashi are that she was poisoned too. They won't have toxicology reports for another few hours. But the autopsy on Juno seems to point to hemlock soaked in oil. Juno still had some left in her stomach."

Hemlock soaked in oil? Hmmm.

"So this is what I suggest we do next." Kayo stood up from her spot and slapped the creases out of her jeans. "First, we should pay a visit to the Sakurai house and size up Nagisa for ourselves. Then we'll visit the grieving family last and hope we don't piss anyone off."

"I know just what we can bring to smooth over the intrusion!" Hana raced off to the kitchen.

Kayo grabbed her purse off the low desk next to the computer and offered a hand to help me up. I threw off the blanket and let Kayo and Akiko boost me up.

"Sorry I'm so slow. I know I'm getting in the way and

making things difficult," I said, as I got my feet under me. Akiko frowned, but Kayo waved me off.

"You're fine, Mei. Let's all get in the car and wait there for Mom."

"Sounds like a plan." I clapped my hands and squealed. This woke up the baby, and she somersaulted so hard that even Kayo and Akiko saw the motion ripple across my belly.

"Wow!" I clutched at my swollen belly and smiled at Kayo and Akiko's wide eyes. "Looks like everyone's ready to solve a mystery today." I winked at them both. "Let's go before she gets impatient. I have my bladder to think of."

CHAPTER
TWELVE

The front door of the Sakurai house opened, and a woman my age poked her head out. Her expression went from perplexed to surprised as she saw Kayo and Hana.

"Kayo? Hey! It's great to see you! It's been forever," the woman said, laughing and bowing. She opened her arms, and she and Kayo hugged amiably. "I thought you lived somewhere in Saitama Prefecture?"

"I do. I returned home for the Fall Matsuri. I didn't want to miss it three years in a row."

"And you brought friends..."

She paused, settling her right hand on her hip. I was sure we were unexpected and possibly in the way, what with preparations for the evening's activities happening in almost every household in the area. There was food to cook, kimonos to lay out, and rooms to be cleaned.

"I did. Nahoko Sakurai, these are my friends, Mei Suga and Akiko Kano." Kayo paused while we bowed, and then, it was as if her mind tripped over her mother. "And you remember my mom, of course." Kayo's lips bumbled over the words like they were made of rubber.

"Yes, of course," Nahoko replied, her expression softening. "Hana, it's great to see you. Everyone, please come in." She gestured us in the door, and with her voice dropped said, "There must be some pressing reason you've made this visit."

We entered her foyer, and while we slipped off our shoes, I noted our surroundings. Nahoko looked like any other young professional, with a shoulder-length haircut and side swept bangs. Her clothes were comfortable and preppy, a pair of wide-leg khaki pants and a black-and-white striped long sleeve shirt. But the worn black leather doctor's bag sitting on the bench opposite the door attracted my attention. I nodded my head to it while catching Akiko's eye. She raised her eyebrows in response.

"Yes, I'm sorry to bother you. I know this is a busy day for everyone in town, especially you."

We walked into a Western-style living room with two couches and a coffee table facing a fireplace with a flat-screen TV over it. NHK was on the TV but muted, a half-finished cross-stitch sat on the couch's arm, and a cup of green tea steamed on the coffee table.

"It's fine. I was just taking a break. I have to go out and do three more house calls before the fireworks tonight. Can I get you all something to drink?"

"No. No, thank you," I said, sitting down on the couch.

"We don't want to be any trouble," Akiko said, joining me.

Nahoko frowned at this. I was sure we were trouble, regardless of wanting to be or not. But this when Hana saved the day and produced a cake from the bag she was carrying.

"I hope you don't mind, but I remembered that I owed you

a cake and the recipe for the cake." Nahoko's face blanked as she stared at the round, bundt cake, drizzled over with icing. Hana slid the cake plate into Nahoko's outstretched hands with a satisfied smile. "I got the pineapple from a friend who just returned from Hawaii. You can bring in the canned variety without having to hand it over at customs. I hope you enjoy it."

"Wow." Nahoko bowed. "I was telling Nagisa earlier that we had no desserts in the house for our guests this evening. But I can't take this cake. It's too rich, too nice."

She tried to hand it back to Hana, but Hana lifted her hands into the air.

"No way. You dropped everything two months ago to come help out with Asami. I promised you I'd get you some of the cake you had that day." Hana turned to us. "Asami was my cat. She was... How old was she, Kayo?"

"About fourteen? An old and cranky fourteen." Kayo huffed a laugh as she sat down. "Nahoko is a veterinarian, and a fantastic one too. She's one of the few who's willing to make house calls for those animals who refuse to get in a carrier."

Nahoko snapped out of her daze and set the cake on the coffee table. "Or animals that are not great at being in a doctor's office," she pointed out, "like all the pigs and cows I see weekly."

A cat came out of the back of the house and twisted up in Nahoko's legs. "Who let you out of the back room?" she asked right before Nagisa called down the hall.

"Nahoko! Mom says she's not feeling well!"

Nahoko sighed. "Mom's on a new medication, and it's not agreeing with her. Please excuse me." She bowed as she left, and we all looked at each other.

Now what?

But Nagisa slipped out of the back room and came out to us. "How nice of you all to drop by and bring cake!"

Nagisa's smile charmed me, along with her ripped t-shirt and old jeans. When we had seen her earlier on the float, she had been dressed in an impeccable red kimono. But here, in her home, she was just a bright, young woman with a warm smile and easy way about her.

"I owed your sister for helping with my cat before she passed away," Hana said, "and I knew you were bound to have people over after the festival. Congratulations on your big debut today in the parade. I bet you're excited for the performance tonight."

My eyes were glued to her, wondering what her reaction would be.

Nagisa's head dropped a bit, and she smiled before she frowned. "Well, I am excited for the performance, but I'm sad about Juno's death." Her voice wavered as she dropped to the floor to sit on her knees. "She taught me so much. I don't know how I'll make it through the performance without her guiding me. I don't know how I'll make it through *life* without her guiding me."

"Oh no, Nagisa," Hana cooed, coming forward to put her hand on Nagisa's. "I'm so sorry you're so upset about this. It is such a shame someone as talented as Juno would die so young. She will be missed. But we all, eventually, move out from under the wings of our mentors. I'm sure you'll fly strongly now on your own. You're more than allowed to miss her and grieve for her, though."

Nagisa sniffed up and pushed her long, straight hair off her shoulder. "I had so much left to learn." She sighed, deflating. "And for Juno to miss the national theater recruiter today as well? It breaks my heart."

"What's that?" I asked, perking up. I had almost fallen into a daydream listening to Nagisa, imagining her with Juno at rehearsals and together afterward drinking saké and spending time together. I knew right away that her feelings were genuine. There was no way this woman could be a murderer as opportune as it was for her to get rid of Juno.

Except maybe it was more than opportunity just for some local celebrity.

"Yes," Nagisa said, sniffing and nodding. "Juno's agent had arranged for a recruiter to be here today and tonight to see the show and Juno perform. I met him today after the parade. He seems to be a very nice man."

That's it? A very nice man?

"Did he..." I waved my hand in a circle, but she just stared at me. "Did he seem interested in your talent? I mean, we all saw you perform today in the parade, and we were quite impressed. I know I was."

"Me too," everyone else chimed in.

She barked out a goofy laugh as she reached for a tissue from the box on the coffee table.

"Oh, I could never take Juno's spot, and he never mentioned me doing as much either. Though he said he would stick around to see how I did in the main performance this evening."

Nahoko came out from the back of the house, and when she saw her sister crying, she came up behind her and set her hand on her shoulder.

The gesture sparked a memory, and suddenly, I let out an audible "oh" and jumped forward. I had been daydreaming about Chisé and needed to know more about her.

"Are you okay? Is it the baby?" Akiko's concern was immediate.

"We've heard you're good friends with Juno's younger sister, Nahoko," I said, ignoring Akiko.

She flinched at the change in conversation. "Chisé? I am. We're good friends, best friends."

Nagisa looked up at her older sister, and this time I didn't see love and trust between them. I saw anger pass across Nagisa's eyes.

"We were only a year apart at school, and we met and got to know each other at film club."

"They're inseparable." Nagisa couldn't hide the hint of annoyance and boredom in her voice. "They'd be together right now if Chisé wasn't at home with her family in mourning."

"Tell me about her," I said, point blank. I wasn't going to hide my curiosity any longer. I needed to know if she would kill her sister for money. Nagisa and Nahoko glanced at each other. "I hear she's a clerk at a convenience store?"

"Yeah." Nahoko straightened up with a smile. "And she's been learning to farm and handle farm business, too. I got her the job at a place just out of town where I take care of their animals." Nahoko's chest rose with pride. "They've been thrilled with her work. I'm so proud of her." She blushed and pressed the fingers of her right hand to her flushed cheek.

"And what about her relationship with Juno? Were they great friends too?"

Nahoko squirmed in her seat and rearranged her legs, right to left, left to right. "Well, no. Not *great* friends. They had their own sisterly difficulties. You know..." She giggled nervously.

Nagisa slid her eyes to the side at her sister. "*We* don't have those problems."

"We're lucky we get along," Nahoko said through a clenched jaw.

"Does Chisé have any debts? Maybe she has expensive taste in clothes or jewelry?"

I knew I was overstepping my bounds as an outsider, so I didn't bother to look at Kayo, though Akiko said my name in warning under her breath.

Whatever. Time was ticking away, and even I wanted to solve this case before the fireworks started. I wanted to go to bed and not have to think about this murder again.

But Nahoko wasn't having any of my meddling. "I don't think that's any of your business." She stood up and looked about ready to chastise me when Hana's phone rang.

"I'm sorry." Hana took the call right in front of everyone. "Hello, Taro!" Her husband was on the other end of the line. "Oh. Oh no. Not again... Okay, we'll be right there."

She hung up and turned to face us. Nahoko was staring me down, and I refused to budge. Something about her, the way she talked about Chisé set my senses tingling.

"We have to go," Hana said, stepping into Nahoko's line of sight. "I hope you enjoy the cake. Please feel free to come by Imagawa anytime, and we'll chat."

"Sure. Fine. Great." Nahoko tore her eyes from me and faked a smile for Hana. "Thank you all for coming. If you'll excuse us, I need to help get Nagisa into her kimono. It takes ages to tie up the obi."

She bowed, and I sneaked past her. I grabbed my shoes and slipped out the door into the warm breeze of the afternoon. Everyone followed me, not wanting to hang around inside for another minute. Thankfully, the front porch was clean and dry and wouldn't ruin my socks.

"Wow, Mei. Way to blow our cover." Kayo huffed as she sat down on the front porch steps.

"I know, and I'm sorry," I whispered. "But you saw how she acted in there. Hopefully, she calls Chisé and tips her off that someone is asking around town about her. I just know these women had something to do with Juno's death."

"And what if you're wrong and we insulted them for no reason?" Kayo asked, her hands on her hips.

"Then I'll beg her forgiveness for you. I happen to be very good at groveling."

Akiko laughed at this, and Kayo threw her hands up in the air. Hana got in the car and started it.

"We have to go now," Hana called out the window. "The police are back at Imagawa, and your father is freaking out."

She revved the engine as we all jumped in.

CHAPTER
THIRTEEN

I t turned out that Hana was just as much of a speedster as her husband, Taro. She was just better at going slow when speed wasn't needed.

Today, speed was needed.

She worked her way to the brewery through every back road on the outskirts of town, staying away from the populated inner-city streets. With the matsuri in full swing and people driving in from all points in the prefecture, traffic was a nightmare. Hana's knuckles had turned white by the time we pulled up to a street two blocks away from the brewery.

"We won't get any closer than this," she said, staring past the police blockades and the squad cars parked in front of the brewery with their emergency lights on. Several uniformed police officers stood guard along the barricades while other busybodies tried to peer past them at the brewery and the chaos there.

And it was chaos. There had to be at least twenty officers milling in and out of the brewery. Forensic vans were parked half in the street and half on the sidewalks, and even a K-9 unit sniffed around the outside of the building.

Kayo had to argue with the guards posted on the street, but they eventually let us in. They had all kinds of arguments for why we shouldn't be allowed to approach the building while they were investigating, but Kayo stood firm. It was her building too, and she had a right to be there. They couldn't argue with that.

A warm wind whipped up the street, and I turned my face down to avoid getting anything in my eyes. October would still bring plenty of sunny days before turning cold in November. The temperature would drop some tonight, so I tried to close my eyes and enjoy the warmth on my face. Thoughts of the two murders loomed over every bit of good humor I could muster though.

I was getting a feeling deep down in my gut, a feeling I frequently had in the past when I suspected someone of murder. Maybe my instincts were specially tuned to people up to no good, or I had a knack for this? I didn't know. I didn't really care. This was my talent, just like painting was at home. I had a sixth sense for crime, and I needed to take advantage of it.

Kayo's shoulders were up around her ears as she walked in front of me. I hustled to meet up with her.

"Are you mad at me?" I asked, trying to keep pace at her side.

"No. Yes. Maybe a little." She sighed. "No, I'm not mad. If anything, I'm angry with myself for getting involved in this in the first place." She stopped to face me. "You know, coming back here isn't easy."

"I get that," I said, keeping my voice soothing. Kayo had a lot of past buried here, most of which I knew nothing about.

She was exceptionally brave. I reached out and grasped her upper arms in my hands. "You're doing a great job. Really."

"Except that's not what I'm supposed to be doing. I'm supposed to be having a nice, quiet weekend with my girl-friends and my family. Not solving a murder."

"I'm so sorry this happened to you and your family. But well..." I shrugged and jerked my head at the Imagawa Brewery crawling with cops. "It's not like you had much of a choice. Your family's business was ground zero for this one."

Kayo's jaw hardened, and I suspected she was grinding her teeth. She always said it was a bad habit of hers.

"It's just that..." She sighed again and relaxed. Akiko turned around from looking in the brewery window and came back. "You don't know what it was like for me when I worked here. I solved more than one murder case here. Me." She jammed her finger into her chest. "Yet Sano or Ichikawa always took the credit. I love that Goro always gives me the credit I'm due back home, but I'm still never included enough to really make a difference."

She bit her lip and threw her hand forward at the brewery.

"This time I *have* to make a difference or my family's liveli-hood will be on the line." She glanced over her shoulder at the crowd forming on the sidewalk. "Because if I don't, you know those people are never going to forget it."

Akiko rested her hand on Kayo's shoulder as I let go. "Try not to worry, Kayo. I feel like we're close to the end of this. We said we'd solve it by the end of the day, right?"

"I said I'd solve it. You all just agreed," she grumbled.

Akiko laughed. "We're as gullible as you are." She slid her arm over Kayo's shoulders and pulled her in for a sideways hug. "Let's go inside."

But we got close enough to the door to see what was going

on between the cop cars parked on the sidewalk and Kayo's back raised up like a cat encountering an unknown dog.

"What the...?" She clamped down on her mouth, keeping the myriad of swear words I knew she wanted to say from coming out.

All the way down the sidewalk, the Kubako police force had laid out the trash from the brewery. They labeled each piece with a number, and an officer proceeded down the length of the sidewalk, photographing every one of them.

"What's going on now?" she asked, and none of the officers acknowledged her. They were all too engrossed in their work to make any concessions to Kayo. "Excuse me! Someone better tell me what's going on right now."

The brewery's door opened, and Kayo's friend, Joy, walked out, her face flushed and a smile upon her lips. The smile died immediately.

"Kayo! Is everything okay?"

"No!" she yelled, and Joy jerked back. "No, everything is *not* okay. Why are you all still here at my parents' brewery, huh? This is harassment!"

Joy's smile slid into a frown, and her expression became stoic. "Don't yell at me. I'm the one who gave you those tips, remember?"

She approached Kayo, and her demeanor was so intimidating, even Akiko and I stepped back. Wow. She was the perfect person for a police officer. Sweet, almost cute and happy looking, and then boom. Fierce.

"Ichikawa is on a rampage, trying to find this killer. He wanted to arrest your father, bring him in." She crossed her arms and got right up in Kayo's face. "I convinced him to come and search the place, search the garbage, search the storeroom. If we found anything, we could arrest him."

"You won't!" Kayo moaned in frustration, her hands balled into fists.

"Of course we won't. You think I don't know that?" Joy's eyebrows jumped. "We're not going to find anything because there's nothing to find."

Kayo let her gaze dip to the ground.

"Come on. You worked with Ichikawa. You *know* him. The only way to get him off a rampage is to —"

"— let him burn himself into the ground," Kayo finished. She paused, and I held my breath. "I'm sorry," she burst out, and I let go of the breath. "It's just... It's never been my family before, you know?"

"I know." Joy softened back into her cute form. It was like watching a Pokémon evolve and devolve. I was halfway into a daydream of her commanding some kind of creature on her shoulder when the door to the brewery flew open.

"Mitsuwara, get in here!" Ichikawa roared at us, and Akiko and I jumped and clutched each other. Kayo and Joy, though, shrugged and followed him in.

Inside, we passed the rows of saké and joined Hana, Taro, and Fumio in the seating area. No one sat though. Everyone stood and faced Ichikawa and his bad mood.

"What's this I hear? You have a suspect in *my* case?" Ichikawa's face was molded into fury, and he breathed like fire was ready to shoot out of his nostrils. "There's no way you have a suspect in my case because *you don't work for me anymore.*"

I glanced past a stricken and pale Kayo to her mother. Hana's eyes were downcast. Well, I couldn't blame her for shifting the attention onto Kayo. Anything to absolve her husband and save the family business, right?

And I would do anything for Kayo. She was my friend, and I took care of my friends.

It was time to grovel.

"Please, Mr. Ichikawa," I pleaded, stepping in front of Kayo, "this is all my fault." I pushed Kayo back a step. "I'm, well…" I lowered my eyes and bowed. "I'm the hothead and irresponsible one here. I convinced Kayo we should help out with the murder investigation. She? She wanted nothing to do with it. It was my idea."

I counted to five before I raised my body. A good shaming always involved a suitable bow.

"And who are you?" Ichikawa's voice raised and his tone was incredulous.

"I'm Mei Suga, sir. I'm a friend of Kayo's from Chikata." I swallowed and tried to force my body not to sweat. The baby stirred, and I put a protective hand on my belly. Not that I thought he was going to hurt me; more that I wanted to remind myself of my situation. Pregnant and involved in a murder investigation.

Mei, you are crazy.

"Suga… Suga… I know that name." Ichikawa rubbed at his cheek, and I panicked. Oh no. He was going to recognize Yasahiro's last name. Maybe he'd give my husband and his restaurant trouble! What had I done? "Wait. The Amanda Cheung murder case. Oh great." His mood shifted to annoyed. "Great! Now I've got some amateur, wannabe detective sticking her nose in my precinct? This is outrageous!" He lifted his face to the ceiling and the veins on his temples throbbed. The man looked on the verge of a cardiac episode.

Kayo and Joy stood there watching, like they saw this all day, every day, no big deal.

Then Ichikawa roared incoherently and stalked past me, straight out the door. The wind gusted up while the doors were open and rustled the posters and papers in the window as he stormed out.

Kayo huffed, and Joy let go of a held breath.

"I didn't expect him to recognize... me?" Since when had my ancillary work on the Chikata murder cases become known several prefectures away? I didn't want to admit it, but I was proud.

"That actually went pretty well," Kayo said, and I blinked at her.

"Yeah. I expected that to go much worse." Joy nodded her head and pressed her lips together.

The door reopened, and Ichikawa stormed back in. Everyone froze.

"You," he said, pointing at Kayo, "are forbidden from interfering in this investigation. Sano has sworn on the record that Juno was fine until a few minutes before she died."

"That doesn't mean —"

Ichikawa cut her off with a raised hand. "Kobayashi was here earlier, eating her lunch and having hot saké before she met Sano and then everyone at the garden, where she died."

I groaned and cursed under my breath. Again a connection to the brewery? I looked across to Hana and Taro, and they, once again, sagged in misery. I wished Taro had kept the place closed for the day, but he'd said the brewery was always a hot spot during the festival. They depended on the sales to help float them through the winter.

What a mess.

"I'm closing this place down, and I'm taking your father and Fumio into custody."

"What?" Kayo yelled, and her face paled. Joy grabbed Kayo's arm. "You can't do that!"

Ichikawa's face settled into stone-cold anger. "Don't you

dare tell me how to do my job. And I swear to the heavens, if you so much as breathe near this case again, you'll join them in jail."

Several officers came in to escort Taro and Fumio from the brewery. They were nice about it though. Taro and Fumio were allowed to grab their coats, and the officers didn't handcuff them.

"Wait," Kayo said, intercepting her father and stopping Fumio on their way out. "What can I do? Did you see what she was eating?" She wiped away a tear that rolled down her face, and my heart broke for her. Kayo so rarely cried. She must have been dying inside.

Her father grasped both of her shoulders and squeezed. "Kayo, no more. Just let the police handle this. I don't want you in jail too." Taro's lips quirked in a sad smile at us, probably feeling meek and embarrassed over everything that had happened. He hastened past us and out the door with his accompanying officer. Kayo watched him go, her eyes full of tears and her face pale and tired.

Fumio walked up next to her. "Whatever it was," he said, cocking his head to the side and aiming his eyes out the window, "it was in a brown paper bag along with sweets from the *wagashi* shop on Takata Street."

Kayo turned to look at him, and he shrugged.

"I always hated to see you cry," he said over his shoulder as he followed Taro out the door.

CHAPTER
FOURTEEN

We waited until Ichikawa drove off with Taro and Fumio before we walked outside to consider the trash on the sidewalk. The tableau of paper and plastic stretched out about three meters down the front of the building, and the forensics officers had trapped several smaller pieces of trash under rocks so they wouldn't fly away in the fall breeze. Far off in the distance, beating drums echoed down the streets, and the high notes of a flute reminded me that today was a festival day for everyone else. The matsuri was in full swing, and we were missing it.

Whatever. Right?

I couldn't let my best friend's family go to jail when I felt in my bones there was no reason for them to be there.

"Takata Wagashi... Takata Wagashi..." Kayo mumbled under her breath, looking up and down the rows of trash. "What if she took her trash with her? We'll never find it!"

We each took a section of the sidewalk and peered past the officers cataloging everything. I made sure to look and not touch, knowing the police would find any reason, any at all, to send us to jail with everyone else. And I couldn't solve a case from prison.

I had some talent for cracking cases, but it didn't extend to solving them just by willpower alone. I wasn't some superhero with x-ray vision or telepathy.

My brain shifted into daydream mode, and I was floating over a bank robbery, flying in a suit and cape. I switched the suit and cape from blue to black and smiled. Yes, I'm definitely more of the darker variety of superhero. If I have to break a few bones to get the bad guy, I'll do it.

"Mei!" Akiko's voice broke into my wandering thoughts.

"Huh, what?"

"Why are you standing there staring into space? I've found it!" Akiko pointed down at the ground.

"Found what? Oh," I said, looking at the trash, "Kobayashi's lunch?"

We all gathered around Akiko including two of the forensics officers. They should've told us to leave the scene, but it seemed that most of them tried to tolerate Ichikawa and his tirades, and no one took him seriously unless they had to. With him gone, we were safe for the time being.

On the ground, between a convenience store bag with two rice ball wrappers in it and an empty bento box, was a clear, empty plastic clamshell with a few pieces of greens sticking to the sides and a pink wrapping paper with "Takata Wagashi" stamped on it. It had probably been wrapped around the small, white cardboard box next to it. I licked my lips, thinking about the sweet wagashi treats which had been in that box a few hours earlier. Knowing the season, they had been maple-flavored. My stomach growled in response.

Kayo grabbed a pair of rubber gloves from a box sitting on

the sidelines, and we all did the same. She picked up the plastic clamshell, opened it, and sniffed.

"Salad with a toasted sesame oil dressing." She handed the box to Joy. "Didn't you say the hemlock that killed Juno was from an oil?"

"Yeah." She sniffed the box. "This smells... strange."

"May I?" I asked, holding out my hand. She gave me the box, and I sniffed. It did smell different, but I couldn't place why. I gave the box back to Joy.

"I'll get this off to the lab right away."

She slipped by Hana who was on her tip-toes trying to see past us to the forensics people and the trash. "Oh no," she said, watching Joy retreat with the clamshell box. "Oh no, oh no."

"What's the matter, Mom?" Kayo asked. Her mom had blanched and pressed her fingers to her mouth.

"Chisé, Juno's sister. I saw her working at the farm stand yesterday afternoon while I was waiting in line for my salad. By the time I got to the head of the line, she was gone for the day. Do you think...?"

Yes! The scene coalesced in my memory, and I saw Chisé, in a handkerchief and glasses, step forward and help a young woman out at the farm stand. I didn't recognize her later at the brewery because she had been dressed differently. At the farm stand, Chisé had handed a cup of salad dressing to Juno, Juno had smiled and waved, and left. Juno was holding the weapon that killed her. She had voluntarily eaten it. It had been given to her by a loved one.

A sharp pain pierced my chest as I took off the disposable gloves and handed them to Kayo. Could this be true? Could a woman really hand poison to her sister and smile about it? That would be pretty cold-hearted. Perhaps she didn't know what she was doing? But then if she didn't, she would've been poisoning plenty of other people too.

Kobayashi was poisoned. How did she fit into this?

"I think..." Kayo paused, squinting at the setting sun down the street.

The sky was bathed in warm, late afternoon light — perfect weather for a festival, a performance, and fireworks. I checked my phone, and it was around 16:00. The sun would set in just over an hour. We only had a little bit of daylight left.

"I think we need to visit the Takagis and meet the family for ourselves." She sighed as she realized all the officers were listening to us. "I barely remember Chisé. I can't judge her based on my memories and what we think may have happened. Especially since Sano is still the likely suspect. He had relationships with both women and was with them both before they died. I don't know..."

"I don't know either. And perhaps... perhaps we should leave this alone," I said, pulling her away from the officers. It was a lie, but I didn't want to show our hand in front of everyone. I leaned in and whispered, "We should get out of here before we say anything else."

Joy glanced over at us as we retreated from the scene, then she jogged to catch up.

"Look, I'm sorry about Ichikawa." Joy walked beside us. "He's such a pain. I wouldn't blame you if you kept on looking into this. Honestly." She held her hand to her heart. "If my father were in jail, you know I'd be out there, chasing down leads."

Kayo looked over her shoulder at the other officers. Two of the men had their eyes trained on us. I pulled my bag closer to my body.

"I'm sorry about yelling at you earlier, Joy." Kayo bowed a

little, but Joy morphed into her cute form and tackled her with a hug. Kayo squeezed her, and Akiko and I smiled at each other. "I won't lie to you. We're going to the Takagi house. I need more information before I can believe that Sano killed Juno and Kobayashi."

"I understand," Joy said, pulling away. "Do what you have to do. But you should come with me first."

"Why? Where are you going?" Kayo asked, but I smiled and nodded. I knew where Joy's next step would lead.

"We need to go check the farm stand first," I said, pulling my phone out. It was only a five-minute walk from here, but I wanted to look at the map again.

"Right." Joy was impressed. "You're quick at this." She pointed to me, raising her eyebrows at Kayo. "I like this one. You should keep her around."

Kayo laughed, and the sound of it reassured me. "Don't worry about that. Mei's not going anywhere."

Joy smiled as she signaled for more officers to join us. It was time to make headway on evidence.

———

THE FOOD STALLS LEADING UP TO THE TOWN CENTER were a mess of people. Old and young, men, women, and children milled about, eating and laughing. The headcount had increased by three-fold from the day before, and now even foreigners were in the mix. I passed a group of four people speaking German and another group with British accents. Or were they Kiwis? This was hard for me to tell. Someday I would make it to New Zealand though. Someday. I had my passport now with one stamp in it from France. Yasahiro promised me we would fill it up.

Since I'd fallen behind Kayo, Akiko, and Joy, I decided to text my husband. I figured he wouldn't text back. It was late in the day on a Saturday, and he'd be at his restaurant prepping for the evening sitting. I imagined him slaving away over a pile of expensive mushrooms, a pot of soup bubbling next to him, and all of his attention on his knife as it sliced and diced.

"What are you wearing right now?" I giggled as my thumbs flew over the screen. *"Seriously."*

He would find that text a few hours from now and laugh.

But my phone buzzed in my hand.

"Sexy chef whites. And they're clean for once. I miss you."

Aw. That's sweet.

"The bed was empty without you, and your belly."

"I bet you loved having all the extra space," I texted back.

"I slept on your side. I hope you're jealous."

"I am. Hey, this case is getting exciting. I think we're actually going to crack it."

"Really? Do you have any guesses about who it was?" He knew none of the details of this murder case, but it was nice that he showed some interest.

"I have my money on someone. I'll let you know if I win the bet."

There was a pause as I wound my way through the crowd and approached Kayo, Akiko, and Joy at the farm stand.

"My money is on you. Always. Text me before bed?" He included a kissing smiling face.

"I will. Later!"

"You want to do what?" The woman at the farm stand asked, her eyes blinking rapidly at the growing line of customers and the police officers approaching from the opposite direction. The banner across the front of the stall read, *"Chisai Tanuki Farms - Organic Produce and Meat."*

Joy held up her police ID. "We need you to shut down your table for the evening, and we're going to have to take you into custody and have all of your supplies tested."

The woman blanched as two officers directed the crowd of customers away and advised them to get in line somewhere else.

"I... What's this about?" She snapped off her food safety gloves and pushed them into the pocket of her apron.

One of her assistants was the same young woman I saw here the previous day. She had been the one to fumble the delivery of salad into Juno's hands. I tilted my head as I looked at her, trying to gauge if she was panicked or worried. Her eyebrows were drawn together in confusion, and she scratched her head, but her breathing was steady. She stayed put, stepping up behind her boss to offer support.

"I need to ask you a few questions about what you serve here and how it's prepared." Joy flipped open her notebook and clicked her pen.

"Uhhh," the woman stammered. "It's just salad." She shrugged her shoulders and gestured to the stacks of plastic clamshells. Their salad came in a variety of sizes — small, medium, and large — and two different varieties. "This one is mostly bitter greens with a sweet dressing. The other is baby greens and mushrooms with a smoky, sesame dressing. Both sell really well... or did." She looked longingly at the crowd of people who had moved on to other offerings.

"Have you ever had a problem with people becoming ill from your vegetables?" Joy asked, and the woman gasped.

"Certainly not! We triple-wash our greens. We've never had a case of salmonella or anything like that."

"I see. Okay. I need to know about who works here with

you in the stand on a regular basis." Joy waited while the woman stared at her.

"What do you mean? It's only ever been my assistant and me." She waved to the young woman with her.

I had to interject. "Wait. I was here yesterday, and I saw someone else working here. She was taller, short hair? A handkerchief on her head and glasses?"

"Oh, you mean, Chisé?" The woman grasped at this information like it was an old and dirty sock she couldn't believe anyone could ever want. "She doesn't work at the farm stand. If you saw her here yesterday, it was because she was delivering produce."

"Yes," interrupted the assistant, "she dropped off more greens yesterday and helped me bundle them into plastic containers. Then she unloaded a shipment of dressing and left."

What she neglected to say was that Chisé had handed over the dressing that Juno had eaten. Was it the salad dressing that had been poisoned?

I slipped past her and plucked a dressing container from all the others. When I opened the container, Akiko's hand rested on my arm. "Maybe we should give it to someone else to test?"

"Of course," I said, staring into the dressing. "I just want to see if it smells the same."

It didn't. This one smelled earthier, smelled, well, normal. I tried to place the scent I had smelled earlier. It had been sharper, like fresh cut grass.

"This is fine, but it's not the same dressing as earlier." I snapped the top back on and handed it to Joy. "Who was here earlier today? Anyone helping in the late morning?"

The older woman swallowed hard as she glanced at her

assistant. I'd seen that look before. This was the look of guilt, the pleading eyes, the down-turned mouth, the shifting feet.

"I told her not to come," the woman said, sighing and looking away. "Her family is in mourning. But she insisted, said it was a matter of duty and honor. So she came to the farm early this morning to help wash and sort greens and make salad dressing. Then she came to the stand and helped serve the late morning customers. I didn't think anything of it."

The image of Chisé showing up early this morning to work while her family sat at home grieving didn't bother me. Most people preferred to work through their grief. I certainly had in the past.

What bothered me was that she had come back to murder again.

Cold, premeditated murder. And she had chosen a police officer too.

A shiver ran up my back as the woman continued.

"I figured she missed the work, she missed seeing her boyfriend, and—"

"What?" Kayo asked, her voice hitting a shrill high note.

"What did you say?" Akiko and I echoed.

She pressed her lips together when her assistant hissed a warning at her.

"She had a boyfriend?" Joy asked.

My muscles tensed as I awaited the answer, an answer I already anticipated deep in my bones. We had guessed this was a crime of passion. We didn't understand whose passion it had been.

"Yeah. At least I thought they'd been dating? He came out to the farm a few times to talk with her while she worked." She paused to think. "Maybe it was more platonic than I originally thought? I saw them close to each other once, and he had grabbed her hand. Honestly, I was happy for them both. For her to date a successful police officer? That was a big thing. But what do I know? I'm just a farmer. I barely come into the city or know any of the gossip. It's just me, the cows, and the greenhouses."

Joy groaned. "I don't think I even need a description, but I might as well take one."

Yep. It was a crime of passion for sure. And Chisé had been getting rid of the competition. She'd wanted Sano all to herself.

CHAPTER
FIFTEEN

Thankfully, the Takagi house was on the way out of town, not closer to the center. If it had been, we'd have had to walk because the city was overrun with cars and pedestrians.

We came to a halt at another intersection as the traffic officer directed people across the street in front of us. I was impressed by the number of young women dressed in kimonos crossing the street with young men, the families with children in tow, and many multi-generational families who streamed in from the west side train station. We were only one hour away from the big performance in the town center, and almost three hours away from the fireworks. Yet everyone was arriving early to eat the local food and go shopping. It really was too bad the brewery was closed. I bet they would've done a lot of business today.

Kayo hummed and drummed her fingers on the steering wheel of the car. Hana had given us the keys and accompanied her husband to the police station. It was the right thing to do.

"This day is not moving fast enough for me." Kayo inched

into the intersection as soon as the police officer had cleared a hole for her. "Something about the entire situation rubs me the wrong way."

"You don't say." I tried to keep the sarcasm from my voice, but I couldn't.

"Ichikawa has always had it in for Sano. Maybe the prospect of finally getting rid of him has sent Ichikawa over the edge?"

She looked over at me as she flicked on the turn signal and waited at the intersection to proceed as soon as the pedestrians crossed.

"I mean, Sano" — she shook her head and laughed ruefully — "he's a total ass and a complete jerk, but a murderer? I would think others could see that too, especially since most everyone likes him more than I do."

I shrugged. "Sometimes circumstantial evidence like this all piles on, and it feels like everything is pointing to one conclusion. I bet, due to Juno's popularity, someone came down hard on Ichikawa to get the criminal in custody as soon as possible. He's probably blind to anything else."

"Still," Kayo continued, pulling into a small side street, "Sano is a cop. One of our own. That's almost more scandalous than having a celebrity killed on your watch."

She shifted the car into park and clutched the steering wheel as she stared out at the Takagi home. The house was a dark wood, two-story home with a garden, nestled back into trees and a bamboo thicket. There was one car in the driveway and all the windows were closed.

"Did she kill her?" Kayo whispered, looking at the house. "Was it premeditated? My god, who could kill their family like that?"

"There's only one way to find out if that's the case." Akiko leaned forward from the backseat. "We have to go in and size her up."

We exited the vehicle and slowly walked to the front door, smoothing out our clothes we had been running around town in all day. I thought about the last thing I ate and wondered when I'd eat again. But that made me think of the cake Hana had brought to Nahoko and Nagisa's house. Maybe we should've stopped and picked something up for the Takagis, as a way to soften the rudeness of our visit?

"Listen," I warned Kayo as we approached the Takagi house. "Let's not forget that these people lost their prized daughter yesterday, and they will not be happy to hear you asking about their other daughter. We need to tread lightly here."

Kayo stared at me like I'd grown another eyebrow. "They just carted my father and Fumio off to jail, and you want me to go easy on them?"

Her attitude was incredulous, but I understood it. In my mind, our problems trumped the Takagi's, but death and mourning were not to be taken lightly. People would do anything to protect their families. Just like Kayo would do anything to protect hers.

She turned and stalked up the front walk to the house, and Akiko and I chased after her.

"On second thought, maybe we *should* leave this alone, Kayo. Let's go out for coffee or something?" Akiko did her best to get through to Kayo, but she wasn't listening. With Joy back at the precinct trying to make a new case to Ichikawa, trying to free Taro and Fumio, we had no one to help us but us.

And Kayo was so furious. There was no stopping her.

"Just..." I grabbed her and made her look at me. I mimed taking a deep breath and blowing it out slowly. She closed her eyes and did the same. Okay, good. We were getting somewhere.

I rang the bell, and we waited for someone to come. And waited.

The door opened, and Chisé Takagi stood before us. My first impression? How did this woman kill anyone? She was skinny and a bit homely. If she was wearing any makeup, which I doubted, she was going for a natural look. Her hair was ragged and hadn't been cut in a long time. Sano had been dating her? Really?

"Can I help you?" she asked, looking at us all.

"Hello," Kayo said, relaxing into a reassuring smile, "I'm Kayo Mitsuwara, and these are my friends, Mei Suga and Akiko Kano. We heard about... what happened to your sister and we wanted to come by and express our condolences."

Chisé hesitated for only a moment, then stepped aside. "Oh, please come in. My mother and father are out right now, taking care of Juno's... Anyway..." She choked up a little and hung her head, but she recovered quickly. "They've been so upset. Absolutely beside themselves. I don't know what more I can do."

"I'm sorry to hear that," I said, kicking off my shoes and following everyone into a living room at the front of the house. The TV was off, but Chisé had been sitting at the low family table, drinking hot coffee and studying from a textbook. "I think it's important to just be there for them."

We all sat down at the table, and once again, I wished we had brought something to offer to eat. Because then I'd be eating. My stomach growled.

"So, how did you all know my sister?" Chisé started off the conversation naturally like she'd had to do it day in and day out her entire life. And maybe she had. Perhaps she'd always been outside of her sister's circle of brightness, asking people how they knew Juno instead of why those people had come to see her.

Kayo took the lead. "I knew your sister from school." She clasped her hands together on the table and did a great job of acting the part. I needed to nominate her for an Academy Award.

"You did? Were you very close? I don't remember seeing you around."

I made eye contact with Kayo, trying to warn her. Ugh, this would go downhill quickly if she wasn't careful. We should've rehearsed a story or something before we walked in the door. We should've been better prepared. But nothing about this weekend had been normal or expected. And from what I knew, Kayo was not the greatest liar. She was one of the most truthful people I knew. Acting was one thing. Lying was another.

"Will you be having any services for your sister in the coming days?" I asked, but Chisé was not swayed by my distraction.

"You all look familiar..." Chisé furrowed her eyebrows and looked to Kayo again.

"We weren't very close or anything, but I really liked her," Kayo continued. "She often came to my parents' brewery in town back when I used to live here, and we'd spent some time together, occasionally."

I had no idea if any of that was true, but congratulations to Kayo for digging up *something* to talk about.

"The brewery? The Imagawa brewery?" Chisé asked, her eyes widened. Uh oh. "My sister drank saké from there and died." She brought her hand to her chest and looked at us all.

Oh no. No no no. This was the wrong thing to say. "Actually, I remember seeing you all there last night."

This was going wrong, horribly fast. She'd caught on to our scheme within a blink, and now we had to scramble.

"We were there, yes," I said, taking a right turn. "We felt awful for your family after seeing what happened first hand. We thought we should come to pay our respects."

"How did *you* know my sister?" She turned her attention entirely on me. Now it was my turn to squirm.

"I'm sorry that I didn't know your sister at all. She seemed like such a kind person." I lied, trying to pull on the five seconds of observation I'd had the day before.

"Really talented," Akiko chimed in. "We saw Nagisa play earlier today, and if she was Juno's understudy, Juno must have been extraordinary."

"Juno was arrogant and conceited," Chisé bit out. "And you would've known that, like everyone knows, if you had ever even met her."

"I knew her," Kayo said, pressing her hand to her heart. "And I don't remember her ever being mean to anyone."

Chisé was not convinced. She picked up her phone and tapped away at it. "I believe I have somewhere I have to be. You know, for my sister."

Akiko and I stood up, but Kayo stayed put. "If she was so conceited and arrogant, how did you ever put up with it?" Her voice was low, and Chisé leaned in to hear her better.

Chisé pressed her lips together. "With lots of patience. It doesn't matter now, though, does it?"

It was as though a cold wind had whipped through the room.

"You work at Chisai Tanuki Farms, right?"

Chisé froze in her spot.

"We spoke to your boss just an hour ago about what you do for them there. She said you like to wander the property when you're off the clock and come up with new recipes for their salads and dressings."

Chisé did indeed have an abundance of patience. She thawed and smiled.

"I love to cook and test new recipes all the time. Would you like to try some of my new dressing? I think you'd love it."

Red and white lights raced across the living room.

"I think we'll pass," I said, turning my eyes to the window. Just through the blinds, I could see the police cars with their lights on sitting outside.

My heart leaped. Joy had come to the rescue! She had convinced Ichikawa of Chisé's guilt, and soon this whole thing would be over. I glanced at my phone's screen. And we would be done way before our deadline, too.

Maybe I'd be eating a decadent dinner soon, watching fireworks, and soaking in the hot spring tub before passing out in bed. The baby liked this idea and gave me an excited dance, ready for her own downtime. Goodness knows she'd had her fair share of adrenaline today too. It had been tiring for us both.

"We know what you did," Kayo whispered as Chisé's eyes grew to full saucers.

"What are you even talking about? I've done nothing," she countered, and she was so confident about it, I faltered.

A sharp knock at the door silenced any more conversation. Chisé stormed past us to the front and opened the door.

"Can I help you, officers? This house is in mourning, and we'd prefer not to be disturbed." Chisé's voice sliced through the air.

"We're so sorry to bother you, Miss Takagi." I recognized this voice. Ichikawa. "I'm looking for Kayo Mitsuwara."

I looked over at Kayo and Akiko. Panic made us look for other exits, but Kayo shook her head, defeated.

"Her car is here, so I thought she may have come by to..."

"Pay her respects?" Chisé asked.

"Possibly," he conceded. "Or possibly to question you."

"Please come in." Chisé stepped back into the living room, this time with Ichikawa at her side.

"As I suspected, you just can't keep your nose out of other people's business... out of police business." Ichikawa approached Kayo, and she raised her chin despite the situation she was in. I wanted to raise my fist and yell, "Fighting!" at her.

"Ichikawa, we were only here to —"

"I don't care what you were here for. You could've been here to bring the lady a cake, and I would still call it interfering. And after what Joy just told me back at the precinct, I *know* you're interfering."

Chisé's lips twitched, and anger practically burned a hole in my chest.

"We wouldn't have to interfere if you listened to us." The statement burst from my lips before I could stop it. My hand flew to my mouth. Did I really just say that?

"Mei," Akiko growled at me through gritted teeth.

Yeah, I'd just said that.

Ichikawa's face reddened from cherry blossom pink to temple gate red. Everyone took a step away from him except Kayo. She aimed to deflect him by edging into his line of sight.

"Maybe we can take this outside," Kayo suggested, turning and bowing to Chisé. Ouch. I was doubly aware of how much that cost her, showing respect to someone we believed to be a murderer, someone who eliminated all of her competition and the man who cheated on her as well? After all, Sano was still in jail.

And it looked like Kayo would be joining him.

We followed Ichikawa and his officers outside, where Kayo handed me the keys to her car. Ichikawa handcuffed her and pushed her, gently, into the awaiting cop car.

"I told you not to interfere," Ichikawa said as he slammed the door on her.

Tears formed in my eyes as I watched her being driven away.

Ichikawa ignored us, got in his car, and left. At the door to the house, Chisé smiled, but her smile never reached her eyes. She took out her phone from her pocket and dialed as she closed the door on us standing in the street.

"Now what?" Akiko asked.

I sniffed up and let out a long breath. If Kayo wasn't around to solve this case, then I had to do it myself.

I jingled the car keys at Akiko. "Now it's time for a stakeout."

CHAPTER
SIXTEEN

The car door opened and Akiko slid into the passenger seat with a bag bursting at the seams.

"Oh my, it's getting crowded out there," she said, setting the 7-11 bag on the console between us and slamming the door shut. "I got lots of great food I'm sure you'll love."

"Yes!" I pumped my fist. "Nothing says stakeout like junk food and sitting in a car for hours on end."

"Well, first of all, this is not entirely junk food." She pulled out several rice balls and a package of heated fried noodles with chicken and vegetables. "And we've only been in the car for thirty minutes."

"Indulge me, will you? It's been a rough weekend."

"Yeah, how does that keep happening?" Akiko asked, handing me a cold bottle of water. I plucked one of the rice balls from the bag and opened it. Mmmm, my favorite. Tuna and mayonnaise.

"I don't know," I said around a mouthful of rice. I kept my eyes trained on the end of the street Chisé Takagi lived on. It was a dead-end, so the only way she could get out was to leave the way we came in. I had driven far enough away for Chisé not to notice us then sent Akiko out to buy supplies. One of us had to be here to keep watch, and the convenience store was only two blocks away. "I leave to go on vacation, and everything goes wrong." I shrugged. "I must be cursed."

"Your honeymoon was successful though," Akiko pointed out as she dug into the bowl of fried noodles.

I smiled, remembering the trip to Paris. "It was, but I think it was because Yasahiro planned it, not me. Me? I'm horrible at this."

"But you didn't plan this. Kayo did." She paused, staring out the window. "I guess we shouldn't count on her to plan vacations again after this either." She sighed. "I hope they're treating her well at the jail."

I wolfed down the rest of the rice ball and reached for the second one. "I'm not worried. They're just locking her up to keep her from interfering in the investigation. It's not like they arrested her as a suspect." I stopped to think this over. "At least, I don't think so. If they still believe her dad poisoned Juno and Kobayashi, then..." I shrugged. I guessed anyone in the family was fair game.

"But if they're smart, they'll realize Kayo had means and opportunity, but no motive, right?"

I smiled at her. "Look at you, being all detective and stuff." I reached over and lightly punched her on the shoulder. She laughed, and it made me laugh too. Laughter had been so scarce this past year, for her and me, and it felt good to get in some now. Even with our friends in jail.

I sighed. "It's good to sit and enjoy the little moments, right?"

"It is," she agreed, "and just think, you'll have a lot of that coming up soon with the baby too." She eyed my belly. "Is everything okay there?" The nurse in Akiko couldn't stop doing her job.

I stopped stuffing my face to rub my belly, and I felt like my little girl high-fived me back. "All is well. This is one of the few things going right lately."

"You and Yasahiro are good?" She cringed. "I hate prying."

"You're not prying," I assured her, pleased she wanted to know. "You're my best friend..." She cringed again. "You *are*. I know we've had a rocky year, but I promise. I'm not holding anything of what happened in my heart for keeps."

We had been friends and neighbors all of our lives until we'd graduated school. After years apart from high school through college, we had rekindled our friendship over the past year, through thick and thin. It hadn't been easy, but I felt like we'd made progress.

Akiko, on the other hand, was having trouble with what had happened that brought us back together. She wrestled with her guilt daily, but I was here to remind her that all was forgiven.

I glanced up the street again. Nothing.

"Yasahiro and I are great. We're thinking of names. He wants something that will be nice in both French and Japanese. A hard task." I slowed down my eating as I continued to think of names, but nothing was coming to me.

"Oooh, yeah. That's a tough one. Oooh!" She gasped as I dug through the convenience store bag looking for more food.

"Thought of one?" I asked, looking up.

"No! Look!" Akiko pointed and Chisé's car, the one that had been parked in her house's parking spot, stopped at the corner of her street and turned right on the road leading out of town.

"All right," I mumbled, shifting the car into gear. "That was only about forty minutes. I wonder what she was waiting for." I pulled the car into traffic and followed her several cars back.

"I don't know." Akiko placed the top back on her noodles. "Let me see what's in this direction on the map."

She pulled out her phone and turned on the maps app. Our location was a little blue dot traveling out of the central part of town.

"What's out here?" I kept my eyes on the road in front of me and Chisé's car in the distance. She made a left turn onto a country road and sped up. I tried not to worry that she was so far ahead. As long as I kept her in sight, we should be fine.

"Uh, a chiropractor's office." We sped by the building. "A post office. A candy wholesaler."

We both watched that building go by wishing we could stop. At least, I wanted to.

"And then farms. I bet she's going to the farm she works at to hide the evidence." Akiko's voice climbed, sure she was right.

"I wouldn't be surprised."

We followed her out several kilometers, a bus between our car and hers for most of the way. It was a thankful coincidence. She turned right again, and I slowed down, so we were farther away from her.

"Yep!" Akiko tilted her phone to face me. "Chisai Tanuki Farms. It's up ahead another kilometer on the right. Slow down. We can pull off soon and go in on foot."

I pulled off in a wooded area, just before the cow fields. There was a small parking spot here for three cars and one place left open. A marker on the side of the road pointed to a hiking trail.

"I bet this is where people come to hike to a higher location and watch the fireworks." I parked the car and pocketed the keys.

"I'm sure only the locals know about it, too," Akiko said, nodding. "Good cover."

The sun was setting, and the light had changed to shades of red and amber. A slight chill had overtaken the air, and I pulled my wrap cardigan out of my bag and put it on. Bugs buzzed in the long grass as we crouched and ran through them.

"Maybe we should've checked to see if the farm offices were near the front of the property?" I asked, following Akiko.

"They were. I could see the buildings on the map."

Score ten points for Akiko.

We sneaked along the cow fence, aware we were barely covered, but there was a barn ahead we could hide behind and go from there. Akiko led the way, and we made it to the barn without being seen.

"Phew. Thank goodness we ate something, or I'd never have the energy to do that," I whispered at Akiko.

"The end of the day is grueling," she agreed. She peeked around the corner and snapped back. "Jackpot!" She waved me to the corner.

Chisé was dragging two bags of trash to the back of her car...

And Nahoko was with her.

"Are you sure you got everything?" Chisé asked her.

"I... I don't know. I don't really know what you did." Nahoko dropped a second bag of trash next to the first while Chisé popped the trunk of her car. "But I got everything you told me to get."

Chisé hauled the bags up and dropped them into her trunk.

"What are you going to do?" Nahoko asked. I squinted my eyes at her, and she looked more exasperated than scared.

"Exactly what I said I'd do." Chisé slammed the trunk and turned to Nahoko. "Listen, everything is going to plan. I promise. Your sister is now the star, and mine is gone for good. Now, it's just us."

Chisé took Nahoko's hands, held them, and pulled Nahoko to her.

I nearly gasped as I watched the two kiss. I lost my balance, and my hand slammed against the wall. Akiko squeaked and yanked me back.

"What was that?" I couldn't see Chisé, but she sounded alarmed.

Akiko grabbed the back of my cardigan and tugged me away from the edge of the barn. In a sheer dose of good luck we so sorely needed, a cow trotted up to the fence and mooed at Chisé and Nahoko.

"That one likes me." I could hear the humor in Nahoko's voice. She was a veterinarian, after all, and probably knew all the animals on this farm.

Akiko and I remained quiet, waiting to see if we were caught.

"You and your animals," Chisé teased. "Nahoko, stop worrying. Everything just needs to blow over, and we can start dating again. They all think that detective did it."

I strained my ears to hear Nahoko's reply, but I couldn't catch it. Just the words "didn't think" and "they'll know" and her sister's name.

"I know you're scared, but don't worry." There was a silence here, and I imagined them being intimate again. Sigh. My crazy imagination made it really vivid. "I have to get home.

My parents will be done setting up Juno's funeral soon, and I have to pack before they return."

Okay, of all the things I thought of regarding these murders, I did not see this coming.

So, Sano really was framed? Did she choose him because he spurned her? Or was that all a misinterpretation from the owner of the farm? Maybe it was unrelated to anything.

But with Chisé and Nahoko in a romantic relationship together, the possibilities of their motives unfolded in front of me.

Nahoko would want to see her little sister succeed at what she did best, and Chisé, wanting to make her lover happy, would do anything to give that to her if it meant getting rid of her over-achieving big sister. Yes, yes. This was the perfect motive. I had the murder motive down to love; I just had the wrong lover in the equation.

"They're leaving," Akiko hissed at me. "We need to hide."

Car doors slammed, and when the car engines roared to life, Akiko and I ran for the back side of the barn. This end of the barn was mostly open to let the cows in and out when they were allowed to roam free, so we ran around and into the open space as the two cars followed each other down the farm's gravel driveway and turned back towards town.

"They'll see our car." I grabbed Akiko's arm, but she shook her head.

"We parked with other cars. They won't notice it as they speed by." She eyed a cow that had come to check out the people in her barn. "Did Chisé say she was going to pack?"

I huffed in frustration. "Yeah, she must be leaving town. What should we do?"

"It's going to be dark soon," Akiko said, peering up at the sky.

I made a split-second decision. "Let's search the farm and see if they left behind any evidence. It sounds like Chisé expected Nahoko to clean up after her. Perhaps she forgot something."

Akiko looked at her phone. "We're running out of time. Okay. Let's do it."

CHAPTER
SEVENTEEN

There were no other cars at the farm, so we guessed that everyone was either at the farm stand, still being questioned by the police, or in the city awaiting the fireworks. Chisé and Nahoko had met here in a clandestine fashion, anyway, which assured me we wouldn't get caught as we searched the place.

Akiko and I slinked in the direction Chisé and Nahoko had come from, past the main office building and around the back to a more prominent building with a steel door.

"Let's check in here." Akiko went straight to the door and opened it, and I jumped forward trying to stop her before she barreled into private property and got us all in trouble.

"Stop!" I hissed at her and sighed as I gestured to her hand on the door. "You're leaving your prints everywhere."

"Oh," she said, frowning at the doorknob. She secured the door between her feet and wiped off the doorknob with her shirt. "Better?"

"I guess? I don't know. I was always given gloves whenever

I went into a crime scene." I used my foot to take the door from her and followed her inside.

This area appeared to be a prep kitchen for all the food the farm sold. They had been selling salads and dressings at today's festival, but they had ovens and a large stove here too, industrial size, the kind you'd see in a school cafeteria. Perhaps they baked pies or loaves of bread as well during other seasons?

"Here," Akiko said, handing me some food safety gloves from a box on the side counter. I snapped them on so I could start searching.

"We should take them with us when we leave. I know the police can get prints from inside gloves if they need to." I opened the refrigerator, and it was stocked on every shelf.

"Oh really? How do you know about that?" Akiko crouched down to read the contents of the tubs stacked under the large stainless steel prep table in the middle of the kitchen.

"I've been... um, learning..." I hadn't admitted to anyone but Yasahiro that I was spending a stupid amount of time researching police procedures and methods online. I knew it was a stupid idea. Stupid to think any of the information I found was accurate. Stupid to think the internet was a valid source of information. Stupid to be spending my time doing it when I had paintings to paint or people to take care of.

Stupid. I kept repeating that word to myself even as I googled another thing and went down that rabbit hole, over and over again. I was this close to buying second-hand textbooks online about criminal procedures and spending all my extra time at the precinct grilling Goro about whatever forensics experiment I had heard about on YouTube the previous day. I had done almost all of my research in English, to add to the level of difficulty. My brain had been expanded by knowledge and shrunk by pregnancy hormones. It was difficult being in my own head some days.

"Learning," Akiko drew out. She sounded skeptical.

I pulled bottles from the fridge and looked around and behind them. Lemon juice, ponzu juice, coconut milk — nothing here was out of the ordinary.

"I'm not finding anything here," I said, ignoring Akiko's questioning stare.

"Yeah, everything here is fine too." She put her hands on her hips as she swiveled and looked around. "It seems to be an average kitchen."

"And it looked like Nahoko had taken a lot out in the trash." I sighed as I closed the fridge. "I don't think we're going to get lucky this time."

"Wait!" Akiko pointed to a door off the kitchen labeled, *"Trash | Recycling."*

I shrugged. "Sure. Let's go dumpster diving. That's definitely how we should end the day." I pouted as I thought of all the food and desserts I was missing at the festival.

"Now, now." Akiko opened the door and gestured me in. "Going through the trash and recycling is going to be *fun*, I promise."

A ginger cat bolted out of the space between our legs, and I gasped and jumped so high, the baby actually got mad and punched me in the bladder.

"Eeek! Ow." I rubbed my belly while Akiko pressed her hand to her chest. "That cat took off fast!" I panted to catch my breath. "Want to bet it got stuck when Nahoko was here?"

Akiko nodded, heading to the burnable trash first. I remembered that the salad dressing bottles were mostly glass. Could it be that Nahoko had recycled the bottles instead of washing them and reusing them? She was technically a doctor, but the idea of reusing the bottles may have given her pause. It certainly gave me pause. I'd have rather recycled them too. I would've been happier to get rid of them instead of holding onto them and accidentally poisoning someone else because I didn't wash them thoroughly enough.

I sifted through the recycling and thanked my lucky stars that the people who ran this farm were of the neat and tidy variety. The vast majority of recycled glass was beer bottles, and I had to dig past them to find anything.

But I did find something.

"Look," I said, pulling out a salad dressing bottle similar to the ones I saw in the fridge. I hesitated, but I brought the lip of the bottle to my nose. Yes! It was the same sharp, cut grass scent I had smelled in the salad dressing container that Kobayashi had eaten from.

"This is it." I handed it to Akiko.

"Are you sure?" She smelled it too. "*Hoo!* That's strong." She hummed as she looked at the bottle then rubbed her gloved finger along the inside. "It's oily," she said, showing me her finger. "And I bet it's enough for the forensics labs. Do we take it?"

A flash of white burst across my eyes as my heart rate increased. No. The police could see this as tampering with evidence, trespassing, breaking and entering, theft! I didn't want the case to go downhill because of our mistake.

"No," I snapped, grabbing the bottle from her. I looked down at the recycling container and eyeballed where I had unearthed it from, then I placed it back there. In the process, I saw one other bottle that may have held the same oil.

This was plenty of evidence, including whatever she had in her car, to put them in jail. Maybe, if the police dug some more, they'd find texts or emails about the whole situation, too.

But I wanted to pinpoint one more thing.

"It's still a little light out. Let's go out back."

We made sure everything looked exactly as we found it and sneaked out the back door of the building. I pulled my phone from my pants pocket, glad I had it with me. I had left the rest of my bag in the car.

"I hope I get reception out here," I mumbled, holding my phone up in the air. Thankfully, I got a solid two bars, enough to download video from YouTube.

"What are you doing?" Akiko laughed at me.

"I have no idea what poison hemlock looks like, do you?" I raised my eyebrows at her. "I saw it once earlier today on a website on my phone, but that was it."

"You have a point. So we're gonna stand here, trespassing in the middle of some farmer's field, and watch a video on what poison hemlock looks like as the sun goes down?"

"You have a point as well." I squinted up at the sky. "My phone has a flashlight on it. We'll use it if it gets dark. And the video is only three minutes long."

We both hunched over my phone and watched a man describe what poison hemlock looked like, the shape of the leaves and the purple blotches on the stalks. He said he always saw it growing away from other plants, usually at the edge of fields.

I looked towards the cows. I was sure the farm owners would keep the hemlock away from their livestock. I googled and nodded at the search results. Yeah, cows could die from eating a small amount. This was a tidbit of knowledge Nahoko would know as a vet. Maybe she told Chisé about it at some point.

Looking at the cattle fields, the farm owners had cleared the land at least a meter and a half around the fenced-in areas, leaving only grass within reach of the cows. The light was fading fast, but it looked like there were tall grasses and weeds on the other side of the cow field and fence.

"Over there," I said, pointing into the distance.

"Are you tired yet?" Akiko asked as she followed my lead.

"Exhausted. You?"

"Pretty much, yeah."

Five minutes of walking later, my suspicions were confirmed. With my phone light turned on, Akiko and I found the hemlock right along the edge of the cleared field and at least two meters from the cow fence. The shape of the leaves was correct, and there were purple marks all along the stalks.

"Look," I said, gasping as I saw the ground cleared next to the bush we found. The grass had been tamped down here by boots, and a large hemlock bush had been cut away, its broken stub of a stalk sticking out of the ground. "Someone came and got one of the bushes."

Akiko slowly shook her head and smacked away a bug. "It could've been the owners of the farm. You know, hemlock is not native to Japan. Maybe they were doing their best to eradicate it so it wouldn't become an invasive species."

"Yeah. It's only shown up in a few prefectures, including this one. If they were trying to clear it, why didn't they take it all?" I rubbed the dirt from my palms off on my jeans.

Akiko shrugged. "Maybe they ran out of time or manpower? I don't know. But you're right. Your theory makes more sense."

The sun had almost entirely set, and the first stars of the night twinkled above us.

We were so close to solving this case! We had a good idea of the suspect, the means, motive, and opportunity. Chisé even had the evidence *in her trunk.* But without an in with the local police, and Kayo in jail, we were stuck.

What could we do?

Kayo's voice popped into my head. *"I always liked Joy. She's a good person. Very reliable."*

"I think... I think we need to ask for help. What did you think of Joy? Would she help us?" I started walking back around the short way to the car. Hopefully, we'd be back inside, away from the bugs within ten minutes. I knew my blood was tasty, but I didn't want to become a feast. I wanted to eat, not be eaten.

"I think she's our only choice now. It's a good thing I liked her."

"I agree." I handed Akiko the keys. "You drive. I'll talk."

CHAPTER
EIGHTEEN

Kubako was absolutely packed. With 10,000 people who come to see the fireworks annually jammed into the city, everything had crawled to a stop. Akiko inched the car forward every few seconds, doing her best to mine her brain for the most creative curse words she could find and mutter them under her breath.

"Ooh! That was a good one. I haven't heard that one in a long time." I clapped as she smiled and sighed.

"This is an impossible amount of traffic. You know what?"

She gave up, slapped on the turn signal, and threw the car into a U-turn when she found an open parking lot with available spaces pass by.

"We're a kilometer from the Takagi house. Time to walk," she declared, exiting the car and getting the parking lot pay stub.

I tried not to groan as I levered myself from my seat and then the music hit me. When we were in the car, I thought I'd heard drums, but I figured it was the cars next to us blasting their music.

Akiko and I both turned in the direction of the music and frowned. Off in the distance, above the tops of the buildings, the sky glowed and the sounds of singing, flutes, and drums bounced off the surrounding buildings. This was one of the biggest festivals in the prefecture, requiring months of preparation and millions of yen in donations. Every inn and hotel in the area was sold out, and the trains coming to town were packed. And now the big performance was happening, and we were missing it.

"I wanted to see the big matsuri show," I said, folding my arms over my chest. "And I especially wanted to see Nagisa play."

"Wasn't the whole show supposed to be awesome?"

"Yeah. They have a huge musical number they do and a play about this famous monk's life. I hear it ends with forty people on stage doing a simultaneous dance."

Akiko remained quiet for a moment. "Weren't we supposed to be on vacation? I put my dog in an expensive kennel for all of this. What a waste of a weekend off, right?"

My stomach clenched. The last thing I wanted was Akiko mad at me over what happened this weekend, and I could hear it in her voice. She needed this weekend away as much as I did, and now it was ruined. Ugh. I felt horrible about it. Her friendship was important to me, and it was hard won over the past year, for both of us.

"I'm sorry," I said, waddling up to her side. My hips ached in protest, and I winced in pain. "Ahhh, ouch." I stopped to stretch them, and Akiko stopped with me. "My body is not used to all this exercise."

"May I remind you that your body is carrying another human being?" She looked past me to a spot up the street.

"Maybe you should go to that café up there and rest, and I'll take care of this."

"Oh no." I straightened up and readjusted. The baby had hiccups again and was fluttering in my belly like a well-timed metronome. "I'm not leaving you to handle this alone. This is all my fault. I should see it out to the end."

Akiko rolled her eyes and led the way at a slower pace. "You have to stop doing that."

"Doing what?" I kept pace at her side.

"Trying to take the blame for everything. This mess, of course, is not your fault. It just happened, and we've been dealing with it the best we can."

"It wasn't my fault? But I was the one who thought solving the crime would be fun."

"We would've been involved in any case because Kayo's family was involved. So, once again, not your fault." Akiko stomped onward. "Just because you feel bad about what happened with your mother and the house and the typhoon and everything doesn't mean you're to blame." She threw her arms out, and I dodged to avoid them. "This martyr attitude you've developed is getting old. Stop letting people walk all over you."

I nearly tripped over my own foot. "Me? A martyr? You must be joking." I laughed, but Akiko did not.

"I see it more and more from you lately. You apologize a lot for stuff that's not your fault. You should stop. It doesn't suit you."

If I had said at any point that I loved Akiko for her bluntness and can-do attitude, then I took it all back.

Seriously.

She sighed when she looked over at me. I was sure I looked

harassed and annoyed. I could feel it in the corners of my mouth.

"Hopefully, now that I've said something, you'll pay more attention."

Whatever. I kept my mouth shut, and we walked in silence the rest of the way as I churned this thought over and over in my head.

When it came to the old ways, the ways of my mother's generation in Japan, I tended to shun them. I'd gotten pregnant before my husband and I married, and I didn't do the ridiculous amount of education that everyone else did, with the office job and the high-rolling city life. I'd tried that, and it sucked. My life was not something for me to be proud of. But between my mother's disappointment in me and my repeated failures to do anything right in the last year, I had started to shoulder the blame for everything to keep the peace. It made everything easier for everyone else even if it made my own life difficult.

Akiko was right, of course. It took me less than a kilometer to admit it too. What would I do without her?

We rounded the corner for the Takagi house and found a police car parked out front. Joy was standing on the front porch, speaking with an older man and woman. They were both pale and disheveled, and I guessed they were Juno and Chisé's parents.

"I'm telling you, there's no way she would've left like this. Her sister's wake will be tomorrow after her body is returned to us. We —"

The father broke down in tears, and the mother hugged him. Joy shuffled back and forth, uncomfortable in her own skin. She lit up with relief as we approached.

"Thank goodness, you're here," she whispered. She

excused herself from the bereft couple with numerous bows and kind words and met us in the front garden. "I got here, and the Takagis were in distress. Chisé left a note." She handed over the piece of paper she clutched in her hand.

It read, *"Mom and Dad, I'm so distraught over the death of Juno that I'm going away for a few days. I can't even bring myself to be there for the funeral. Hopefully, when I return, the police will have found her killer, and I will be able to visit her in peace at her final resting place. I still think the Imagawa Brewery had something to do with it. Please convince the police to search their building again. Perhaps they didn't find every-thing the first time. I love you both, and I'll call soon. Chisé."*

I ground my teeth so hard my jaw hurt. "That's so low."

Akiko read it and had to stop herself from throwing it in the dirt.

"I swear to you that we're right about everything we saw," I pleaded with Joy. I dropped my voice even lower so Chisé's parents couldn't hear. "Chisé and Nahoko did this together. There's evidence still at the Chisai Tanuki Farm, and in the trunk of her car." I looked past the house, and Chisé's car was parked in the spot in front of her parents' car. She had arrived home first, wrote the note, and split on foot.

"Did you ask to search the car?" My voice wavered as I thought about how much time we were wasting. If Chisé was on foot, she could be on a train and halfway to Tokyo by now.

"No. Let's do that right now."

Whatever Joy told the parents, they agreed to the search right away. She popped the trunk, and it was empty. Where did the evidence go? We saw her put it in the trunk.

Joy's eyes shifted left and right, left and right. She was considering all her options. What was next?

"I have an idea."

She returned to the parents, reassuring them with whispered words and calming gestures. They nodded and headed back inside their house as Joy bowed and waited for them to close the door. She snapped up and ran through the garden to us.

"Imagawa Brewery is ten blocks from here. We need to go there now. I think we're only about fifteen minutes behind Chisé." She patted her officer's uniform and found her phone. "See here," she said, pulling up the maps app. "This is Imagawa, and then another ten blocks this way is the train station." She began to walk as she looked at her phone again. Akiko and I followed without comment. "Hmmm, the next train out of here doesn't leave for another thirty-five minutes. We may catch her. Let's go!"

She began to run, and I panicked. No way was I running pregnant. I was a runner before I became pregnant, and I jogged in my first trimester. But not since then. With my tea shop located right under my apartment, I didn't have to go many places, and I could be lazy when I wanted to be. Akiko wasn't much into exercise either, to tell the truth, but she grasped my arm and nodded.

"I'll keep up with her. You walk."

She ran after Joy, and I hustled to catch up. The real irony of my whole situation was that everything was great when I was on the move. My muscles would sing, and my step was light and quick. The minute I slowed down, everything seized up, my joints became stiff, and my muscles ached.

I wondered if this was the pregnancy or me. It had to be the pregnancy.

I speed-walked past people on the street absorbed in their phones or talking with their companions and wondered what would await me at Imagawa Brewery. Was Chisé too fast for us?

When I turned the corner and saw the brewery up ahead, its dark state momentarily perplexed me. Right. Everyone who worked there was either at the performance or in jail. Akiko emerged from the side alley and waved me towards her.

"Guess what?" Akiko's smile was a kilometer wide.

"Chisé dumped the evidence in the trash here," I said, panting and rubbing at the stitch in my side.

"That's right!"

"Lucky guess." I winked at her and approached Joy who was bent over bags of trash. Yeah, these were the ones we saw Chisé store in her trunk not long ago. She had loaded her evidence into plain, combustible trash bags instead of in the proper recycling bags. I had to bet this was a deliberate attempt to call out the difference and pique the interest of the police when they came to investigate the matter further.

Nice try, Chisé. But we're on to you!

"You're sure this is what you saw her put into her car truck?" Joy was taking photos of the bags with her phone.

"All trash bags look alike, you know? Can you dust it for prints?"

"Yep. And the brewery has security cameras." She pointed up at the corners of the building. "Including the businesses up and down the block. We could probably trace her all the way back to her house." She sighed as she looked up and down the alley. "People always forget about how safe it is in Japan because we make it safe. Underestimating law enforcement and the willingness of people to help the police are the biggest mistakes most criminals make."

She was right. Most people would help the police if they were asked. I knew I would.

"What's next?" I asked, bouncing on my toes. I could feel it. We were close to catching her.

Lights from a police car bounced up the alley, and Joy waved her hand at the car parked in the street.

"Forensics is coming back, and that's your ride to the train station."

"Let's go!" An angry voice roared up the alley, and Akiko and I both ducked.

Ichikawa stood outside his car, glaring at us, and I could feel the heat of his anger from five meters away. Eek. He was not happy at all.

"Get your interfering butts over here right now!"

Akiko and I ran as fast as we could.

CHAPTER
NINETEEN

chikawa's driving skills rivaled that of Taro Mitsuwara. He raced down streets, blasting his siren, lights flashing, and never once hesitated to hit a turn at full speed.

"You and Taro Mitsuwara must be the best of friends." I clutched at every available safety bar, even bracing my feet against the sides of the footwell.

"I don't have any friends." Ichikawa jerked the steering wheel and came to a grinding halt as a mother and her three kids crossed the street in front of us. A traffic officer ushered them across the crosswalk and signaled us to go. The tires squealed as we took off again. "And I'm not looking for help at the office either. I told you earlier today I don't want anyone interfering in this case. And you just couldn't listen."

Anger burned my cheeks. Excuse me? He was still going to hammer on at me about interfering in this case?

Akiko's words from earlier about quitting the martyr complex echoed in my head. The right thing to do here was to apologize. That's what he wanted. This man was all about dominating everyone around him until they obeyed every order he gave. He was in charge, and he knew it. Everyone else knew it too.

No. Nuh-uh. I wasn't having it.

"Excuse me?" I put as much attitude as possible into those two words. Ichikawa turned down a new street, and the train station loomed up ahead. People ran from the street as he approached, and he leaned over and switched off the siren but kept the lights flashing. "You're not going to thank me for helping you out on this case? Because as far as I can tell, between Kayo, Akiko, and me, we caught your murderer, and if we hadn't gotten involved, you'd still be barking up the wrong tree."

He came to such an abrupt halt, the seatbelt nearly choked me. I coughed and rested my hand on my belly. The baby was still hiccuping. Wow, she was calm in almost every situation. I hoped that continued through birth and beyond.

"A thank you for helping out would be nice right about now." I tried to keep my cool, but my frustration had leaked through.

Ichikawa shot me a look that could kill a small animal, opened the door, and let himself out.

"What a rude bastard," Akiko whispered.

We jumped out of the car and followed Ichikawa into the train station. Other police cars joined us from different directions, and Ichikawa muttered instructions into his radio at other officers in the area. "I need coverage at every exit and inform the local railway chief that we need service halted for ten minutes."

There was a burst of static. "Railway chief's not going to be happy about that."

"Remind him this is a murder investigation and then send him to me if he gives you any trouble." He clicked off the radio and grumbled under his breath about timetables and reputations. I rolled my eyes without him seeing. No one liked it when the train was late, but everyone was polite about it if circumstances were terrible.

"Suspect spotted on the eastbound platform... Make that both suspects." The radio crackled as we entered the station and the railway employees waved us through the gates.

"What were they wearing?" Ichikawa asked me.

"Uh... Um..." I thought about what I had seen at the farm before the sun went down. "Chisé looked the same as when we were in her house. Light pink shirt and jeans. Black shoes. Nahoko was wearing wide-leg tan pants and a black-and-white striped top."

Ichikawa ran up the stairs to the platform while Akiko and I rode up the escalator. I was not running up any stairs.

We arrived on the platform, and my line of sight landed on Chisé. The recognition lit up her eyes. I was in a place I wasn't supposed to be again. First, it was her house. Now it was the train station instead of down by the beach for the fireworks, which was where everyone else was going.

Chisé turned to Nahoko, whispered in her ear, the two picked up their bags, and started walking in the opposite direction. Ichikawa kept his eyes on them and pursued at a calm pace. Had they been running, I felt sure he would've run as well. He didn't want to spook them, and I couldn't blame him. The train station had multiple levels and exits, and it was possible all the ways in and out weren't covered.

Akiko and I increased our pace. I wanted to be there when the police caught these two. For once, it wasn't me versus the killer with my life on the line.

Wait. What was that?

A gust of wind and a train horn pulled me up short. I glanced at Akiko, and her eyes widened at the same time.

A train was pulling in. Ichikawa broke into a run as the train glided into the station and stopped at its designated spot. Chisé and Nahoko were halfway up the platform now, and her satisfied smirk made my blood boil. She was going to get away.

"I said no trains!" Ichikawa yelled into his radio as the train doors opened and people streamed off.

Chisé and Nahoko didn't wait for others to disembark. They pushed into the train and disappeared into the masses of people still trying to make it into town before the fireworks.

We caught up with Ichikawa as he frantically peered into the windows of the stopped train. The radio crackled to life. "Railway chief was overruled by corporate. The train was too full to keep it stopped outside of the station. They said they'll hold it here, though."

"Arrrgh!" Ichikawa cried out as he pushed past people to get on the train. Had he even seen the direction Chisé and Nahoko went in? What if they had split up?

I imagined them jumping from the other side of the train and disappearing along the tracks into the darkness. My heart pounded as I considered their options. They would get away, and we'd never see them again.

So close! We were so close to catching them, and we were failing.

Akiko and I stood back from the crush of the crowds exiting and flowing down the platform, and I reached out to grab her hand. Sadness washed over me. All the work we had done was about to be for nothing.

People swirled around us, as many people as I experienced in a typical Tokyo rush hour, and a young man bumped into me, turning me around.

"Oh, I'm so sorry. Excuse me," he said, bowing and continuing on.

My line of sight went past him to the escalator we had just come from. Chisé had stolen someone's jacket and tried to disguise herself, but Nahoko wasn't as lucky. Her crazed and alarmed eyes searched the area for police as Chisé pulled her along, keeping her head down and her stride long.

"There," I said, pointing, and Akiko took off with me right on her heels.

I wish I could've seen her face because grown men cowered and shrank away from Akiko as she raced away from me. A path opened up before her, and she must have pulled strength from the deepest reaches of her body to close the distance between Chisé and us.

Chisé and Nahoko were halfway down the stairs when Akiko reached the top. The station chimes played, and I grasped for the handrail to steady myself as I watched Akiko take the stairs two at a time and snag Chisé by the collar.

"Yes!" I called out. "Ichikawa!"

The station chimes drowned out my voice, so I shouted for Ichikawa again. Chisé screeched and pulled her arms from the stolen jacket. Nahoko tried to help her escape, but she tripped and skipped down the stairs on her butt then rolled to a stop at the bottom. She cried out in pain, and Chisé's face paled.

This gave me enough time to call for the police again, and this time they came running. Akiko let go of Chisé, but there was no place for her to go. Police were everywhere, and several officers streamed past me on the stairs to grab Chisé and take her into custody.

"Nahoko!" Tears cascaded down Chisé's face. "Is she okay?" Chisé struggled against the hold of the officers.

Nahoko groaned and rolled over. I breathed out a sigh of

relief. She was probably bruised and battered from that fall, but she'd be fine. Since she wasn't trying to run, the police kept her lying on the floor, unwilling to injure her further. One of the men pulled off his jacket and slid it under her head. The gesture sparked a sad smile on my face. Even criminals would still be treated like people.

Ichikawa finally ran up next to me and hooted a big breath as he observed the mess of officers and suspects on the stairs below us.

"Great job," he said, and the compliment surprised me. But I guessed nothing made the man happier than catching the killer on the run.

He actually smiled at me, and so I smiled back. "It wasn't me. It was Akiko. She was a lot faster than I could ever be in this state."

I waved to Akiko who was talking to one of the officers, reciting her version of the events. She waved back, smiled, and wiggled her hips in a victory dance. I laughed.

"Well, I suppose I do owe you a thank you," Ichikawa said, gesturing to descend the stairs next to him. "And I think I have a way to repay you. Come with us to the police precinct." He checked his watch. "It's almost time for the fireworks. We'll let Kayo and her family out of holding, and you can all watch the fireworks show from the precinct rooftop. Best view in the city and a hell of a lot less crowded."

With Chisé and Nahoko in custody and my friends about to be released from jail, I couldn't think of a better thing to do.

"That's the best idea I've heard all day."

CHAPTER
TWENTY

The trunk of the car slammed closed, and our luggage awaited us next to the passenger side. Though I had been at the train station only about twelve hours ago for a police chase, I was happy to be there again, this time to head home.

"Thanks for the ride to the train station, Mr. Mitsuwara," I said, bowing. "And thank you for driving just a bit slower this time, too." I smiled as I realized how much of a stretch that thanks was. Had he driven slower? It was hard to tell from the manic cries and people dodging out of the crosswalks as we blazed through them.

"Please, call me Taro. After what you did for us, I think we should be on a first name basis." He opened his arms for a hug, and I was surprised to find us all, Akiko, Kayo, and me, in his arms. The man was a hugger. I had no idea. He patted our backs and let go to step back and stiffen up again like the hug was something he would never admit to. I found the whole thing endearing. "Hana and I are forever in your debt."

"Dad..." Kayo rolled her eyes.

But she softened with a huffed sigh and let her mother adjust her hair and jacket. This was something I begrudgingly allowed my own mother to do to me, even though I was well into my late twenties, married, and pregnant. Mothers never stopped being mothers even if their children were old or gone.

"Thanks again for booking us at the inn and everything." Akiko grabbed her bag and mine. "Please tell Manari and Utako Haségawa again how much we enjoyed our stay at the Haségawa Inn. That place was just lovely. I hope we'll get to return someday and stay there again."

"They would love that, I'm sure," Hana said, bowing her purple head. Purple was the color of the day with a fuzzy purple backpack and purple platform shoes as well. I loved her sense of style. It was a little jarring at first, but it had grown on me quickly.

We all turned around as a car sped up to us and blocked in Taro and Hana's car. Fumio parked, grabbed bags from the front seat, and joined us.

"Oh good, I'm just in time. I didn't want to miss saying goodbye." He bowed to Akiko and me before handing us each two bottles wrapped in beautiful *furoshiki* cloths. "These are my favorite bottles of saké. Just a little gift to say thank you and I hope you'll come back again someday."

"Thanks!" I beamed at the gifts. "I love saké, so I'll hold on to these until after the baby is born."

"Yes, right," he said, bowing again. "We wish you the best with childbirth and a happy baby."

He knew all the right things to say. I smiled and raised my eyebrows to Kayo as Fumio bent down to get one more bag and hand it to her.

"This is for you. Thank you for not giving up on the investigation, even when things were dire... Even when you ended up in jail right next to us."

Kayo took the gift and directed her eyes at the ground. She wasn't one for blushing, but she couldn't make eye contact if something embarrassed her. When she lifted her head, she was back to all-business.

"I was just doing my job. And I would always do everything I could to protect my family and the brewery." She nodded to Fumio, and he took the statement in stride. I wasn't sure if he had been looking for a change of heart from her or what, but Kayo hadn't forgotten he was the one to end their relationship. Not the other way around.

Still, Fumio smiled at us and turned his head when a train horn blew in the distance.

"Sounds like your train is approaching. Let me help you get your bags inside."

Kayo's parents and Fumio saw us all the way into the station, and the station staff pointed and waved at us as we bought our tickets and scanned them at the gates. Despite the crowds from the night before, most people were sleeping in and taking the day to see the local sites. The station was not too crowded.

We said our goodbyes and made it up to the platform with ease. I flashed back to the night before, chasing our killers down the stairs and handing them over to police. Had that really happened? It seemed like a dream.

"Next time we want to go on vacation, *I'm* doing the planning," Akiko insisted as the train pulled up.

"I'm definitely not doing it ever again," I said, with a laugh. I rolled my bag into the train and down the aisle. Akiko lifted it into the carrying rack for me.

I sat down next to Kayo, and she was looking into the bag

Fumio had given her. She smiled and set the bag at her feet, not saying what was in it. I would be lying if I said I wasn't curious. What was in the bag?

"Now, ladies." Kayo opened her carry-on bag and removed three bottles of green tea and a surprise package of sweet cakes. "Let's make it home in one piece. Chikata awaits our return!"

We opened our bottles, and each reached for a cake.

It had been quite a weekend, and I couldn't wait to go home.

THANK YOU!

Thank you so much for reading *Matsuri and Murder*. I enjoyed traveling to someplace new and meeting new people! I hope you did as well.

If you want the next book in the series... You can read *The Daydreamer Detective Finds Her Calling* next!

Please leave a review of *Matsuri and Murder* wherever you purchased it. I welcome all reviews positive or negative. Reviews are so important to both authors and readers.

Want news of upcoming books, events, or free stuff? Subscribe to Steph's mailing list at https://www.steph gennaro.com/subscribe/

If you want more books like this one, you can check for more books on my website at http://www.stephgennaro. com/books/

FROM STEPH

HELLO, READERS!

Prior to the beginning of May 2018, I had no idea I was even going to write this novella for you. In fact, I didn't see myself writing in this world again until late 2018! But I was contacted by a friend and fellow cozy mystery writer and asked to submit a novella to the Destination: Murder box set. This box set would have novellas that take place in countries all over the world, and they thought I would be a good fit for the set. I was intrigued! I have never added any of my Miso Cozy books to any box sets, so this would be a first. But after thinking about what I would write for a few days, I rose to the task!

It was a lot of fun planning and writing this novella. Not only would I have to take my normal novel length and pare it back to a mere 40,000 words, but I also had the added task of introducing characters I hope to put in a new series in 2020. So I hope you enjoyed Kayo's parents, the brewery, Fumio, and all of Kubako, because this is not the last you'll see of them!

But I have to say that my favorite part of writing this book was that a good portion of it was written while I was in Japan at the end of May 2018. I wrote on this while sitting in my hotel rooms in Tokyo, Kanazawa, and Kyoto, in between moments of sightseeing and eating. *Matsuri and Murder* will always have a special place in my heart because of that.

Thanks again for reading!

A NOTE ABOUT CHANGES TO THIS BOOK

In case you missed it in the Foreword...

In Japanese, the most common way of showing respect to another person's social standing is with the use of honorific suffixes that are appended on the end of either first or last names. The most common, -san, means either Mr., Ms., or Mrs.

In earlier versions of this book, and in the whole series, I did use these honorific suffixes. But for 2019 and onward, I have switched to the English way in order to make this series more accessible to English speakers. I hope you enjoy this version!

The town in this novel, Chikata, is completely fictional, though the area I put it in is not. Saitama prefecture is located to the west of Tokyo, and many of the eastern areas are considered to be suburbs of the city. Chikata is located farther out west, nearer to the prefectures of Nagano and Gunma.

ACKNOWLEDGMENTS

Big thanks goes out to all the people who helped or inspired me with this book including...

- Tracy Krimmer.
- Charity Vandehey.
- Germaine Fletcher.
- Cori Wilbur.
- Lola Verroen.
- Anne R. Tan.
- All those in my favorite FB author groups.
- My brother, Brendan.
- My mom, Claire.
- My husband, Keith.
- And my two girls, C and D.

ABOUT THE AUTHOR

Steph Gennaro is a long-time Japanophile, and she's been studying Japanese culture and language for over 20 years. She loves dreaming of far-off places, going for walks with her dog, Lulu Ninja Assassin, hanging out with her family, and reading outside in the summertime. There is no better season than summer. She's a Capricorn, mother, knitter, and web developer, and pasta is her favorite meal. Steph Gennaro is her pen name for cozy mysteries, but she also writes science fiction romance and many other genres.

Find her online at...
www.stephgennaro.com

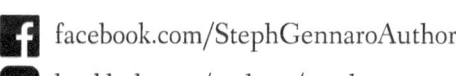

facebook.com/StephGennaroAuthor
bookbub.com/authors/steph-gennaro